A NOVEL INSPIRED BY THE LIFE OF
GUIDO D'AREZZO

MUSIC'S GUIDING HAND

Kingsley Day

THE
MENTORIS
PROJECT

Mentoris Project
745 South Sierra Madre Drive
San Marino, CA 91108

Copyright © 2022 Mentoris Project

Cover design: Karen Richardson and Jim Villaflores

More information at www.mentorisproject.org

ISBN: 978-1-947431-48-5

Library of Congress Control Number: 2022936029

All net proceeds from the sale of this book will be donated to the Mentoris Project, whose mission is to support educational initiatives that foster an appreciation of history and culture to encourage and inspire young people to create a stronger future.

Publisher's Cataloging-in-Publication (Provided by Cassidy Cataloguing Services, Inc.)

Names: Day, Kingsley, author.
Title: Music's guiding hand : a novel inspired by the life of Guido d'Arezzo / Kingsley Day.
Description: San Marino, CA : The Mentoris Project, [2022]
Identifiers: ISBN: 9781947431485 (paperback) | 9798201258573 (ebook) | LCCN: 2022936029
Subjects: LCSH: Guido, d'Arezzo--Fiction. | Music theorists--Italy--History--To 1500--Fiction. | Monks--Italy--History--To 1500--Fiction. | LCGFT: Biographical fiction. | Historical fiction. | BISAC: FICTION / Biographical. | FICTION / Historical / Medieval. | MUSIC / Religious / Christian.
Classification: LCC: PS3604.A9867 M87 2022 | DDC: 813/.6--dc23

The Mentoris Project is a series of novels and biographies about the lives of great men and women who have changed history through their contributions as scientists, inventors, explorers, thinkers, and creators. The Barbera Foundation sponsors this series in the hope that, like a mentor, each book will inspire the reader to discover how she or he can make a positive contribution to society.

Contents

Foreword

First and foremost, Mentor was a person. We tend to think of the word *mentor* as a noun (a mentor) or a verb (to mentor), but there is a very human dimension embedded in the term. Mentor appears in Homer's *Odyssey* as the old friend entrusted to care for Odysseus's household and his son Telemachus during the Trojan War. When years pass and Telemachus sets out to search for his missing father, the goddess Athena assumes the form of Mentor to accompany him. The human being welcomes a human form for counsel. From its very origins, becoming a mentor is a transcendent act; it carries with it something of the holy.

The Mentoris Project sets out on an Athena-like mission: We hope the books that form this series will be an inspiration to all those who are seekers, to those of the twenty-first century who are on their own odysseys, trying to find enduring principles that will guide them to a spiritual home. The stories that comprise the series are all deeply human. These books dramatize the lives of great men and women whose stories bridge the ancient and the modern, taking many forms, just as Athena did, but always holding up a light for those living today.

Whether in novel form or traditional biography, these books

plumb the individual characters of our heroes' journeys. The power of storytelling has always been to envelop the reader in a vivid and continuous dream, and to forge a link with the subject. Our goal is for that link to guide the reader home with a new inspiration.

What is a mentor? A guide, a moral compass, an inspiration. A friend who points you toward true north. We hope that the Mentoris Project will become that friend, and it will help us all transcend our daily lives with something that can only be called holy.

—Robert J. Barbera, Founder, The Mentoris Project
—Ken LaZebnik, Founding Editor, The Mentoris Project

Preface

More than a thousand years after the death of Guido of Arezzo—also known as Guido Monaco (Guido the Monk)—his influence remains pervasive. As the inventor of music notation, he created a method of specifying pitch using the lines and spaces of a staff, a system still used universally today. He also devised standard syllables for the steps of the musical scale, an innovation that is famously celebrated in the song "Do-Re-Mi" from Rodgers and Hammerstein's *The Sound of Music*.

Yet, aside from his authorship of four surviving works of music theory, the documented facts of his life are scarce. Even the date and location of his birth and death are uncertain, though local tradition places his birth in Talla, a small town north of Arezzo in north central Italy.

The principal source of information about Guido's life is his own *Epistola ad Michahelem*—a letter he wrote to Michael, a friend and fellow monk at the Benedictine abbey of Pomposa, located in northern Italy near the Adriatic coast. It was as a monk at Pomposa that Guido developed a new way of notating music as an aid to train singers. But his innovations aroused resentment at the monastery, so he took a new position further inland, training the choirs at the cathedral in Arezzo. Under the patronage of its bishop, Theodaldus, he began putting his ideas in writing, and his *Micrologus* became the most widely circulated music treatise of the Middle Ages. He also collected his written-out chants in an antiphoner, with all pitches notated precisely on a four-line musical staff. To explain this new notational system, he provided the chant book with two introductions, one in prose (*Prologus in antiphonarium*) and one in verse (*Regule rithmice*). The *Micrologus, Prologus, Regule rithmice,* and *Epistola* were widely copied and have all survived; there are no extant copies of the chant book.

Word of Guido's methods reached Rome, and he was summoned by Pope John XIX, who was so impressed with Guido's system that he asked him to stay and teach the singers there. But the area's summer heat and vaporous swamps adversely affected Guido's health, so he presumably went back to Arezzo, planning to return to Rome the following winter. The abbot at Pomposa, having repented his earlier opposition, invited Guido to come back to the abbey, and Guido at least hoped to do so, especially in light of clerical graft at the Arezzo cathedral.

It was soon after his Roman sojourn that Guido wrote his *Epistola* to Michael, who was still at Pomposa. In the section titled *Ad invendiendum ignotum cantum*, Guido outlines his latest innovation, a system using the syllables beginning each phrase of the chant *Ut queant laxis* to identify the notes of the scale: *ut re mi fa sol la*. (In later centuries, *ut* was changed to *do*, and *si* or *ti* was added as the seventh scale tone.) Another medieval pedagogical device, using the fingertips and joints of the left palm to indicate the notes of the scale, became known as Guido's Hand or the Guidonian Hand. The device is never mentioned in Guido's own writings, although it is attributed to him in Sigebert of Gembloux's *Chronicon sive Chronographia*, written roughly half a century after Guido's death.

Documents at a Camaldolese monastery near Avellana, east of Arezzo, indicate that Guido later served there as prior. Beyond these few details, the rest is speculation.

Chapter One

THE CLAY TAKES SHAPE

The gentle hum of the potter's wheel was barely audible above the cries of pain.

Carefully shaping the clay with his hands, prodding the wheel with a stick whenever it began losing speed, Duccio did his best to ignore the piercing screams from the cottage behind him. He knew the midwife was doing all she could to help his wife through the pangs of another childbirth. And he had promised to produce a dozen new earthenware goblets for the manor outside the village, so this was no time to delay his work.

"May the child come quickly," prayed Duccio silently as the screams continued. He knew Ardita was strong—she had already survived the births of their two sons. But his brow furrowed with each cry as he sensed the intensity of her pain. At least the whirring wheel helped distract his mind from something he could do nothing about, and he kept it spinning at maximum speed.

Muscular in build, of medium height, with dark curly hair and a thick beard, Duccio had just entered his fourth decade. He wore the same gray sleeveless tunic he wore every day, a rough woolen garment extending past his knees, accompanied by his usual linen undershirt, woolen stockings, and thick leather clogs. His pottery shed—containing the wheel, shelves for drying and display, and crates for storing glaze and brushes—was a crude wooden lean-to abutting one wall of the family's modest cottage. Just beyond it stood the stone kiln, longer than Duccio was tall, with stokeholes at each end.

A potter like his father and grandfather before him, Duccio expertly worked the whirring mass at the center of the wheel, instinctively knowing just when and how to caress the clay to give it shape. Soon a small cup began to emerge, perfectly rounded and gracefully contoured. In just a few moments it would be time to remove his handiwork from the wheel and set it aside to dry.

From within the cottage, Ardita's screams suddenly gave way to a different cry—the bawling of a newborn baby. Seconds later, seven-year-old Bertoldo, their elder son, ran breathlessly from the cottage to his father.

"Papà! Papà! It's a boy! I have a new little brother!"

"Another boy!" exclaimed Duccio, still concentrating on the spinning clay.

"What will you name him?" panted Bertoldo.

Duccio's mind flew back to his own boyhood, learning the potter's trade at this very wheel from his late father. Without answering his son, Duccio slowed the wheel to a stop, letting the flawlessly shaped goblet come to rest. With the tip of his index finger, he impulsively traced the letters of his father's name on the side of the cup: *Guido*.

~

Nestled in the Casentino mountains in north central Italy, surrounded by wooded pastures, the tranquil village of Talla was four or five hours' walk north of Arezzo, a city known in Roman times for its molded, glazed ceramics. Duccio and his forebears were among the medieval remnants of that artisanship, working the area's distinctive clay to produce earthenware pottery for the villagers and the local nobility. He had already begun to instruct Bertoldo and his younger brother Bernardo in the familial craft, and so later that evening the boys helped their father set out the dozen earthenware goblets for drying—plus the extra one that Duccio had inscribed in honor of the new baby.

A few days later, after the pieces had been glazed and then fired in the kiln, Duccio brought the finished "Guido" goblet into the family cottage—a two-room dwelling with a dirt floor, a thatched roof, and walls made from mud-covered branches. Toward the roof line, tiny open windows admitted a few glints of sunlight, but most of the rooms' illumination was provided by candles.

Duccio was excited to show the goblet to his wife. A petite peasant woman in her mid-twenties with pale skin, full lips, and cascading dark hair, Ardita was wearing her usual long brown woolen dress. Clasping her newborn son as she sat on the straw mattress, she could have plausibly modeled for an artist painting a Madonna and child.

"But what does it say?" she asked hesitantly, seeing the

characters on the goblet but unable to read or write. Even Duccio knew only how to write his own name and his father's.

"It's his name: Guido, just like my father," Duccio answered proudly. "He'll never be a potter himself," he added, knowing he could only bequeath his trade to their first son, or at most to the first two. "But as long as he keeps this, he'll never forget where he came from."

The first week of May found the whole family at the village church for baby Guido's christening. Duccio brought along the goblet, carefully wrapped in a woolen cape, and hesitantly asked the priest if it could be used in the ceremony. The reverend father nodded and blessed it with a sign of the cross.

After Duccio and Ardita formally presented the child and promised to raise him faithfully, the priest immersed tiny Guido in the baptismal font, pronouncing the words of the sacrament. Right on cue, the baby started crying. Smiling indulgently, the priest gestured for the boy's father to dip the goblet into the font. Duccio did so and then tentatively poured a few drops of water on little Guido's head.

"The cup is now a holy chalice," whispered the priest as he restored the squawking infant to his mother's arms. "Treasure it always."

Nodding reverently, Duccio dried and rewrapped the cup. When the family returned home, he carefully set it in a safe place at the back of the highest shelf in their wooden cupboard.

$\sim$

All three boys grew up listening to the hum of the potter's wheel, but for Guido it held a special fascination. From an early age he seemed mesmerized by the sound.

One day as Duccio stood working at the wheel, he heard a small, high-pitched voice humming behind him. He turned to find little Guido—who had barely begun to walk—singing along with the wheel. Duccio smiled as he continued his work, but then he had an idea. He slowed down the wheel so that the pitch of its hum began to drop. Soon Guido was humming lower too, matching the sound of the spinning. Then Duccio gave the wheel a few vigorous turns, speeding it up so that its pitch started to rise. Sure enough, Guido's humming rose higher as well, his voice soaring like a soprano choirboy. Bursting into laughter, Duccio picked up the lad and kissed the top of his head.

"Little Guido," he exclaimed, "I'll never be able to spin the wheel fast enough to make it hum as high as you can!"

Before long, Guido was strong enough to turn it himself. While his father was busy glazing pottery or firing the clay, the boy would stand beside the wheel and try to make it spin with ever greater speed, his delighted shrieks rising in perfect unison with the hum.

"It's too bad he cannot be a potter," Duccio told Ardita. "He hears the music of the wheel."

The wheel wasn't the only music Guido heard. The songs of birds never failed to draw his attention, and he would often imitate their calls. When his parents took him to Mass, even if he was fidgeting, he would stop and listen as soon as he heard the chanting of the priest. And one night, as Ardita was serenading him as usual with a soothing lullaby, she was amazed to hear him begin singing along with her.

She stopped to listen as Guido continued the tune without her. "Do you hear?" she whispered to Duccio. "The boy has music in his heart."

One autumn morning when Guido was still a toddler, the whole family went bustling off to a farm on the other side of Talla. It was the home of Ardita's brother Lorenzo and his wife, who were caring for Guido's dying maternal grandfather. Assorted cousins were milling about the clan's tiny cottage, and there was a feeling of familial affection, despite the sad occasion.

Entering the rear room where her father was lying, Ardita saw a tall, slender man in a black cassock kneeling beside the cot. He was beardless, with the top of his head shaved in a tonsure as a sign of his religious vows. A large crucifix hung from his neck. When he looked up, Ardita cried, "Cristofano!"

He stood, a head taller than his sister, and gave her a brotherly embrace. "Lorenzo sent word that our father hoped to see me one last time," he told her quietly. "The abbot gave me permission to return here for a few days to pay my last respects."

Turning to the boys, Ardita said, "This is your Uncle Cristofano. He's a monk—a holy man in service to God."

Following their father's example, Guido and his brothers bowed their heads.

"These are our sons: Bertoldo, Bernardo, and Guido," said Ardita.

As Cristofano bent forward to greet them, little Guido took a few wobbly steps toward him and grabbed the dangling crucifix, giving it a tug. They all laughed, but later Ardita would remember the moment. Could it have been a sign?

Chapter Two

THE CALL OF THE CHURCH

Duccio and his family kept track of the annual rotation of the seasons, but their specific knowledge of the years' progression was entirely secondhand or thirdhand. Monasteries and wealthy nobles kept elaborate calendars tabulating the days, months, and years, including saints' days and liturgical feasts. Eventually that information filtered down through priests, itinerant artisans, and others who claimed to know. And gradually even the remote village of Talla became aware of the approaching millennium—the year AD 1000, the thousandth year after the birth of Christ.

Talk of the millennium was nearly always accompanied by fearful mutterings: Surely this landmark year would bring the Second Coming of Christ and the end of the world. Monks and other biblical scholars pored over the Bible's Book of Revelation, pondering its reference to those who "lived and reigned with Christ for a thousand years." Some men of wealth and position went so far as to donate all their belongings to the poor and wait for the end.

For Bertoldo and Bernardo, all of this was just another way to tease their little brother, now eight years old.

"You'll never even make it to your tenth birthday," Bernardo taunted Guido.

"Why not?"

"Because the world is about to end," answered Bertoldo with a note of finality.

"Why should I believe that?" asked Guido defiantly. "Besides, if the world is about to end, why are you learning to be a potter? You might as well quit trying."

Unsure how to answer, Bertoldo ran to his mother. "Mamma, Mamma! Guido says the world isn't going to end."

"Guido!" Ardita called sternly as the boys approached. "You know we must all be prayerful and vigilant as our Savior's millennium draws near."

"But the world isn't going to end," Guido retorted. "What could stop the sun from coming up every morning?"

"You must humble yourself before others who are wiser than you."

"Anyone who thinks the world is ending can't be wiser than me."

"Guido, that's enough! No supper for you tonight."

"If I know I'm right, why shouldn't I say so?" he continued, even as his mother escorted him to the ladder leading up to the tiny loft where he slept.

In the end it was Guido who was able to say "I told you so"—although, with the imprecision of date calculations, it was only some weeks after Easter of the year 1000 that the widespread millennial fears began to abate. One Sunday in late April, at Mass in the village's cramped stone chapel, the priest announced that to celebrate the start of the new millennium, a special Mass of Thanksgiving would be offered on the following Sunday at the Cathedral of St. Maria and St. Stefano in Arezzo.

"We must go to Arezzo," said Ardita as the family was returning home.

"It's an awfully long journey just to go to Mass at a different church," answered Duccio skeptically.

"Duccio! This happens only once every thousand years," retorted his wife. "The boys will be able to say they celebrated the new millennium at the big cathedral."

None of the boys had ever heard of a cathedral before, but the occasion sounded exciting.

"Please, Papà, can we go to Arezzo?" begged Bernardo, soon joined by the whining entreaties of his two brothers. Looking at their eager faces, Duccio could only shrug.

And so a week later, equipped with a basket of bread and fruit for the journey, Duccio, Ardita, and the three boys set out before dawn for the long trek down the mountain. Gentry, artisans, and peasants from all around the area were converging on Pionta Hill outside the walls of Arezzo. Tired but excited, the family joined the throng filing across the portico into the cathedral. Although the centuries-old building was in poor repair, the boys gasped in awe as they gazed at the high vaulted wooden ceiling and the twin rows of rounded archways framing the central nave.

More people continued to pour in, and eventually the priests and canons took their places in the elevated chancel to begin the service. The choir was largely hidden from view by a screen, so when a chorus of men's voices began to sing, the sound seemed to come from another world.

> *Te Deum laudamus: te Dominum confitemur.*
> *Te aeternum Patrem omnis terra veneratur.*

Listening with rapt attention, young Guido was transported to a whole new state of being. For the first time in his life, he was hearing the liturgical chants sung not by a single droning priest but by a multitude of trained singers. As his ears drank in the rich, golden voices, Guido little suspected that even greater enchantment was still to come. For as the Mass continued, a hymn was sung by the boy choristers, their pure, sweet voices reverberating into every corner of the nave. It was as if he were being serenaded by angels.

At the end of the service, Guido was still mesmerized by what he had heard. Not even knowing why, but drawn by some inner compulsion, he tried to push forward toward the chancel screen.

"Where are you going?" exclaimed his mother, grabbing him firmly by the hand.

"The music—it was so beautiful," responded Guido, as if in a trance.

"Come along now, we can't let you get lost in the crowd," said Ardita, giving his shoulder a stern tug. But for the boy, even this rough treatment could not undo the spell that the service had cast.

After pausing along the road to eat their modest meal, the family began the hours-long walk back to Talla. Ardita and

Duccio chatted quietly; Bertoldo and Bernardo joked with each other. But Guido walked along in silence, as if replaying the entire service in his mind.

Eventually the path began sloping upward into the foothills of the mountains, and as the trudge became more difficult, the rest of the family gradually ceased their chatter. Only then did they notice that Guido was softly singing to himself. Leaning toward him to pay closer attention, Ardita realized with a start that he was singing a hymn he had heard at the cathedral—intoning every note and syllable perfectly.

Te Deum laudamus: te Dominum confitemur.
Te aeternum Patrem omnis terra veneratur.

Quietly, she caught the attention of Duccio and the older boys, and they all listened in wonder as Guido continued to sing chants from the service's liturgy. The rest of the way home, his parents and brothers walked as quietly as possible, reluctant to disturb Guido's singing.

That night, after the boys were asleep, Ardita reminded Duccio of what had happened.

"He's the third son," she continued. "Bertoldo will inherit your pottery trade, or maybe Bernardo, but never Guido."

Duccio shrugged, unsure where her thoughts were leading.

"And now we know his calling," she said. "His life must be devoted to the Church—especially to music." Squeezing Duccio affectionately as he nodded in agreement, she continued, "The music inside him will be dedicated to God."

~

Having determined young Guido's future, Ardita lost little time in trying to make that future come to pass. She immediately thought of her brother Cristofano, since he was a monk at the Benedictine monastery in Pomposa. If she could get word to him, he might be able to help lead the boy to a monastic calling.

When she shared these thoughts with their village priest, he smiled noncommittally. But fortunately he recalled their conversation some months later when an emissary from Rome arrived in Talla and sought lodging for the night.

"Of course, my son," answered the priest in welcome. "And to where do you journey from here?"

"I am bringing messages from the pope to the Basilica Ursiana in Ravenna and then to the monastery at Pomposa."

"Pomposa," repeated the priest pensively. Within the hour he had sent to fetch Ardita, who soon was eagerly entering his modest rectory.

"You are traveling to Pomposa? To the monastery?" she asked the visitor after the priest had introduced him.

"I am."

"My brother is a monk there. His name is Cristofano. Could you ask for him at Pomposa, and tell him that you've spoken with his sister Ardita?"

"Of course."

Taking a deep breath, she went on. "Then could you ask him if my young son Guido could join the monastery? He's a very smart boy and has a wonderful ear for music."

"I see," answered the Roman emissary. "But does the boy have the proper temperament to be a monk?"

Thinking of her outspoken son, Ardita hesitated. "He is young. He will learn to train his thoughts."

"I will be happy to pass along your request," answered the visitor. "I have other business for the Holy See, but I will bring back word when I am returning this way."

"I'm so grateful," responded Ardita joyfully. She bowed to receive his blessing, then added, "May God grant you a safe journey."

The emissary departed the next morning, and although Ardita reported the conversation to her husband, she said nothing to Guido. His life continued as usual—doing chores for his mother, glazing pottery for his father, and getting teased by his brothers.

Many more months went by before the emissary returned to Talla on his way back to Rome. When he told the village priest about his visit to Pomposa, the reverend father promptly escorted him to Duccio and Ardita's cottage. Summoning her husband from the potter's wheel and sending the boys outside to forage for berries, Ardita seated their unexpected guests before the hearth and welcomed them with an offering of bread and wine.

"Madam," began the visitor, "I have spoken with your brother, and he has spoken with the abbot."

"Yes?"

"As soon as the boy has reached the age of ten, the monastery will be happy to welcome him as an oblate."

Barely able to contain her excitement, Ardita threw her arms around Duccio.

"What does it mean to be an oblate?" asked Duccio, reluctantly admitting his ignorance.

"An oblate is a lay member of the community who is permitted to experience monastic life firsthand," the priest explained. "He will live and work with other oblates, sharing in the life of the monastery to the extent that is fitting. Of course, he is free to leave if at any time you should request his return. When he is older, if he shows signs of an authentic calling, he may take vows to commit to a lifetime of holy service."

Duccio looked at Ardita, whose eyes shone with happiness.

"Thank you both," he said. "We are most grateful."

"And thanks be to God for bringing the Church this new servant," responded the priest as he and the Roman visitor politely departed.

The next Sunday, after returning home from Mass, Duccio and Ardita sent the older boys outside and sat down with Guido in front of the open fireplace. Looking inquiringly from one parent's face to the other, he tried to imagine what in the world they were about to tell him.

"I have a brother named Cristofano," Ardita began. "You probably don't remember, but you met him when you were little, before my father died." As Guido showed no signs of recognition, Ardita smiled and added, "You grabbed for the crucifix he was wearing. He's a monk at the monastery in Pomposa."

Guido still stared back uncomprehendingly, so Duccio interjected, "A monastery is where men go—and boys too—to become monks, to devote themselves to serving God in the Church."

"Cristofano has sent us word that you can join the monastery there as an oblate," continued Ardita.

"What's an oblate?" asked Guido hesitantly.

"Someone who studies and learns to live as a monk. Eventually you will become a novice, and finally you'll be a monk yourself."

"In Pomposa?" asked Guido. "Where is that?"

"Cristofano told us that it lies to the north and east, in Romagna, not far from the coast of the Adriatic Sea," answered his mother.

For a few moments, Guido sat in silence, gazing at the floor. His parents looked at each other, unsure what to say next. Suddenly their son stood up and asked reproachfully, "So you've decided my whole future without asking me?"

Duccio and Ardita exchanged another uncomfortable glance. Finally Duccio answered, "My pottery trade will go to your brothers. As our third son, your prospects are . . . ." His voice trailed off.

"And we've known for a long time that you have a talent for music—a great *love* for music," added his wife warmly. "You'll learn to sing all the chants, just like they sang at the cathedral in Arezzo."

The magical memory of the millennial service suddenly flooded the boy's mind. He took a long, slow breath.

"Fine, I will go," responded Guido quietly. Then he added,

with more than a hint of defiance, "You should have asked me first."

"Guido," said Duccio sternly, "as a monk you must learn to keep your opinions to yourself."

Chapter Three

THE ROAD TO POMPOSA

Although young Guido's days were outwardly the same as always, inwardly he was constantly aware that the life he had led so far would soon be coming to a close. He no longer paid much attention to what his father did in the pottery shed, knowing that his days of glazing earthenware were numbered. And occasionally he let himself slack off when doing his chores around the cottage; after all, soon the family would have to get by without his help.

His brothers had been told the news, but rather than treasuring their remaining months with him, they teased him as relentlessly as ever.

"No wife or children for you, Guido!" sneered Bertoldo.

"No kissing, or hugging, or . . . ." added Bernardo suggestively, waggling his eyebrows.

Guido tried to run away, but Bernardo grabbed him by the hem of his tunic and threw him to the ground. "I'll hold him down and you shave the top of his head!" he screamed to his older brother.

"We'll give you a head start on becoming a monk," joked Bertoldo, wielding a pair of shears.

Luckily their mother discovered them in the nick of time. "Bertoldo! Bernardo! Soon Guido will be going far away," she cried. "This is no time to torment the poor boy."

But torment him they did, fueled by what little their mother had told them about monastic life. "Poverty, chastity, obedience! Poverty, chastity, obedience!" they tauntingly chanted over and over until Guido covered his ears with his hands and ran out into the open fields.

Gazing at the forest, looking up at the mountains, turning back to the cottage and pottery shed, Guido still found it hard to imagine that he would soon be leaving it all behind. How could he live for even a day without the smell of the wet clay, the aroma of his mother's cooking, the fragrance of the flowers outside their door? And how could he even begin to imagine the new life awaiting him? His one consolation was knowing that he would get to sing the music of the Church, like the boys in the choir at the cathedral in Arezzo. He still remembered some of the chants he had heard that day, and only when he was singing them to himself did he begin to feel at peace.

As soon as Ardita was certain that more than nine years had passed since Guido was born, she asked the village priest to check the baptismal records so that she would know when the boy was going to reach the age of ten. The priest reported that he had been baptized in May, so when the next return of that month grew closer, his parents began making plans to take him to Pomposa. Ardita dreaded the prospect of losing her youngest son, but her more practical-minded husband saw the advantage of having one less mouth to feed.

Duccio was able to borrow a donkey from a fellow tradesman for the two-day journey to the abbey. He and Ardita invited Lorenzo's family and nearby neighbors and friends to a modest repast the evening before the planned departure so they could all bid the boy a fond farewell. Even Bertoldo and Bernardo were suddenly nice to Guido, finally realizing they might never see their little brother again.

For Guido, the whole evening was a blur. His mind was already far away, and the repeated good wishes from people he barely knew began to exhaust him. Even so, he was too keyed up to fall asleep and was still wide awake when, as usual, the family woke up midway through the night after their first sleep. This particular night, his parents used the break between first and second sleep to offer special prayers for his future. Only during the night's second sleep did Guido finally doze off, and before he knew it, the cock was crowing.

That morning, after loading the donkey with their supplies for the journey, Duccio did something he had been planning ever since the invitation came from Pomposa. He went to the cupboard, peered toward the back of the uppermost shelf, and carefully retrieved the earthenware goblet he had fashioned the day Guido was born. Blessed at the child's baptism, it was now—at least in Duccio's eyes—a holy chalice. Protectively wrapping it in a woolen cloth and placing it in a leather satchel, he loaded it onto the donkey's pack. Then he summoned his wife and sons.

Gravely, the older boys embraced their parents and younger brother.

"Be good boys while we're away," entreated Ardita as she and Guido mounted the donkey. Then, with Duccio walking along-side them, they began making their way down the path leading out of the village.

After the boisterous gathering of the night before, young Guido found the stillness of the journey a relief. The scant infor-mation his parents had shared with him gave him little basis for imagining his future, but even so, his head was swimming with visions of what might lie ahead. As for Duccio and Ardita, they both had so much in their hearts to say, but no words in their minds to say it with. So they too proceeded in silence.

For long stretches at a time, Guido was able to focus on positive expectations: *I will live at this monastery the rest of my life; I will learn to read and write, I will study, I will work; I will sing, I will pray, I will dedicate my life to God.*

But then less comforting ideas would interrupt his contem-plations. *What if I don't like it there? What if they don't like me? Do I have to do things their way if I know a better way?* Looking from one parent to the other, he was tempted to express his doubts out loud. But something told him that their answers would be no more satisfactory than his own.

And so the trio plodded on through forest and field, from village to village, each step separating Guido further and further from all that he had ever known.

Talla's village priest had directed Duccio to seek shelter for the night with a parish priest he knew in Rimini, on the Adriatic coast. After journeying all day over rough terrain, crossing unawares from Umbria into Romagna, and making multiple inquiries once they reached Rimini, they finally found the well-kept wooden rectory. The priest welcomed them warmly, helped tether their donkey, and then led them to a sparsely furnished upper room for the night. As the candles were extinguished and Guido settled onto a pallet on the floor, he suddenly realized this was the first time in his life that he had slept anywhere other than in his cottage back home in Talla.

Continuing on their way early the next morning, the family stayed close to the shore, where they could see the vast waters of the Adriatic to their right. None of them had ever seen the sea before, and especially for young Guido, the view was awe-inspiring. For long stretches of the journey, the confused premonitions swirling in his head were submerged beneath the sheer sensory experience of watching the play of the seemingly infinite waves.

At last, after passing the lagoons of the Valli di Comacchio, the family turned inland across the plain, approaching the Po Delta. Guido's heart began pounding in anticipation as the road crossed vast fields of green. Finally, in the distance, the abbey's tall, graceful bell tower came into view.

"Look, Guido!" exclaimed his mother.

But he was already staring intently ahead, finally able to see his new home instead of merely imagining it. The closer they came to the abbey, the more distinctly he could see the tower.

Each of its nine levels had wider arched windows than the level below, so that on all four sides, each ascending tier admitted and transmitted more light. The structure's height and unusual design made it seem to soar weightlessly above the surrounding plain.

Within the hour—as the sun began sinking toward the horizon and the bell tower's long shadow was creeping to the east—the family reached the abbey. Brother Valentino, the hosteler stationed at the entryway, offered only a perfunctory welcome, even when they asked for Ardita's brother and explained the reason for their arrival. After directing a servant to summon Brother Cristofano, the hosteler ushered them into an unfurnished parlor, where they waited in awkward silence, overwhelmed by the strangeness of their new surroundings and barely daring to look around. All was quiet except for the occasional echo of passing footsteps.

At last the sound of footsteps grew louder, and finally Cristofano appeared, allowing himself to embrace his sister and then welcoming Duccio and Guido more formally. The boy stared into the monk's eyes, hoping to find some glint of sympathy or welcome, but Cristofano showed no sign of tender feelings.

"You must be very tired and hungry after your long journey," he said flatly, and his visitors did not disagree. "These are our guest quarters," he continued, ushering them toward a small stone building outside the abbey proper. "Our hosteler, Brother Valentino, will help you settle for the night. In the morning you will see the abbey." And with that he slipped away.

Although Brother Valentino's initial welcome had left much

to be desired, the gruff monk now provided them with adequate refreshment and showed them into a small candlelit room with a few mats on the floor. "Here you may take your rest," he said before leaving them.

Exhausted, the parents fell asleep at once. Even Guido, whose thoughts were galloping as he contemplated his new life, could not fight his body's fatigue and was soon sleeping soundly.

The next morning, soon after the morning bells sounded from the tower, Cristofano returned to his guests. "Saint Benedict understood that silence is crucial to monastic life," he said quietly. "The first word in his Rule is 'Listen.' So you will forgive me if I speak as little as possible." Turning abruptly, he went on. "Let me show you around the abbey. From now on, Guido, this will be your world." Accompanied wordlessly by Brother Valentino, they began their tour.

Passing the freestanding bell tower, Cristofano escorted his visitors into the cloister, the rectangular inner court formed by the adjoining buildings. Open to the elements and planted with vegetation in the large central area, it was surrounded on all sides by a wide covered walkway with vaulted ceilings and a colonnade of rounded arches. Strolling from one end of the cloister to the other, occasionally passing other monks at work or in contemplation, Cristofano pointed out the refectory, where the monks communally ate their meals; the dormitory, where they slept; the chapter house, site of daily meetings, lessons, and special rituals; the library, widely famous for its extensive collection; the scriptorium, where monks copied manuscripts; the sacristy, where vestments were stored; the infirmary, where the sick and the elderly were cared for; the kitchen, where meals were prepared; and the lavatorium, where the monks washed their hands before meals. The entire complex was constructed of brown and reddish brick.

Finally, saving the best for last, Cristofano headed back toward the bell tower to approach the abbey's place of worship, the Church of St. Maria. The group entered through the front portico, which was as wide as the church proper; topped by a downward-slanting clay-tile roof, it was fronted by three rounded archways. Then came the family's first view of the candlelit nave: the high, vaulted wooden ceiling; the concave chancel, richly decorated in terra-cotta, marble, and colored tiles; and the long row of rounded arches on either side, supported by ornamental columns. Closer inspection of the walls revealed geometric designs, concentric circles, animal figures, and botanical motifs. Ardita smiled beatifically as she imagined her son's voice reverberating in this sacred space.

Emerging from the dimly lit church into the morning sunlight, Cristofano directed their gaze to the nearby vegetable gardens and the more distant fields for growing wheat, oats, and other crops. "So now," he said simply, "you have seen Pomposa Abbey."

For Guido the tour only added to his fears and confusion. Would he get lost in the maze of buildings? Would all the monks treat him this coldly? Would he have even a tiny corner of space to call his own? The architecture was breathtaking, and the mosaics on the walls were more beautiful than anything he had ever seen. But the atmosphere seemed almost like a prison.

As Cristofano guided them back toward the guesthouse, Duccio and Ardita—reluctant to speak—merely nodded to him in gratitude. Guido was not so timid.

"But where will I learn to sing the sacred chants?" he piped up.

Ardita started to hush the child, but Cristofano restrained her. "I apologize for my omission," he answered. "My duties here rarely take me to the school." Leading the family around the side of the church, he gestured to a separate stone building abutting St. Maria's outer wall. "Here you will learn many things, not just singing—reading and writing, the hymns and psalms, the sacred scriptures, the Rule of St. Benedict."

With a gentle wave, he led them back to the guest quarters. "Brother Valentino will provide you with refreshment. I will return for you when the abbot is ready to receive your oblation."

"Thank you," said Ardita.

"You should know," added Cristofano, "that our abbot's name happens to be the same as your son's. The spiritual leader of our abbey is Dom Guido."

This mention of Guido's name reminded the boy's father of a question he had meant to ask. As his brother-in-law turned to leave, Duccio hesitantly stopped him. "Brother Cristofano?"

"Yes?" said the monk, skeptical that anything on Duccio's mind could merit this interruption.

Opening his satchel and taking out the special goblet, the boy's father continued, "I made this for our Guido the day he was born. It was blessed at his baptism. Perhaps it could be used in the ceremony?"

After eyeing it carefully, Cristofano nodded in assent, then took it from Duccio and quickly disappeared, leaving them in the care of Brother Valentino. For a few moments the family stood in silence.

"I have never before seen such a magnificent place," said Duccio at last, addressing his son. "You are very lucky that this is your new home."

"I hope your life here will be a blessed offering to God," said Ardita.

Guido merely bit his lip, not looking either parent in the eye. Then, without warning, he suddenly rushed to his mother and desperately threw his arms around her.

"Take me home, please! Don't leave me here!"

His parents looked at each other with concern. Valentino turned away as if to pretend he had not heard. Ardita softly patted Guido's head as he sobbed in her arms. Finally he grew quiet and backed away.

"I know I must stay," he said.

Late that afternoon, Cristofano returned and silently led Guido and his parents to the chapter house, where Abbot Guido—in full ecclesiastical regalia—was waiting to receive them. With its lofty arched ceiling and whitewashed walls, the room glowed with the light streaming through its high windows. Resting on a small table was Duccio's chalice, together with a flagon of wine, an ornately calligraphed copy of the Rule of St. Benedict, and a paten bearing the Eucharist. At Cristofano's quiet prompting, Duccio placed the paten in Guido's right hand, then poured wine into the chalice and placed it in his left. As a final step in the preparations, the boy's father wrapped the paten and chalice in an altar cloth. Flanked by his parents, young Guido then stood facing the abbot at the altar, hoping for nothing more than to avoid dropping the sanctified objects he was nervously holding.

After a prefatory prayer—in Latin, like everything else uttered by the abbot—Dom Guido asked, "Who brings this child as a living sacrifice to God?"

"We do," said Duccio.

Next addressing Guido, he asked, "Do you wish to be enrolled as an oblate in the community of Pomposa Abbey?"

Guido's small voice quavered as he replied, "I do."

"May the grace and mercy of God be with you," said the abbot kindly. As he solemnly received the offerings of bread and wine from Guido's hands and placed them next to the altar, he noticed the name on the side of the chalice.

"The boy's name is Guido?"

Both parents nodded.

"And so one Guido welcomes another," said the abbot with a faint smile. Then, placing the manuscript in the boy's hands, he returned to the ritual. "May the Rule of St. Benedict, written in the spirit of the Gospels, show you the true way of Christ."

The abbot next draped a small black cowl over Guido's shoulders and gave a slight downward push. *I guess I'm supposed to kneel,* thought Guido, so he did. Ardita and Duccio followed suit and knelt beside him.

With his hands outstretched over Guido's bowed head, the abbot intoned, "May the blessing of Almighty God come down upon you and remain with you forever, *in nomine Patris, et Filii, et Spiritus Sancti.* In the name of the Father, and of the Son, and of the Holy Spirit."

"Amen," murmured the three.

After a moment of awkward silence, with Guido wondering what, if anything, he should do next, the abbot made the sign of the cross, took the boy's hands, and raised him to his feet. Saying, "May the Lord bless you for this gift," Dom Guido then extended one hand to each parent as they too rose.

Bowing slightly, smiling blandly, and grasping his crosier, the abbot turned and left the chamber.

This time the silence was broken by Cristofano, who had retrieved the chalice. "I must escort young Guido to join the other oblates. You should say your goodbyes now."

Ardita was caught off guard, not expecting the separation to occur so immediately. She could scarcely choke back her tears.

"Duccio," continued the monk, "here is the chalice you provided for the ceremony."

"Might the boy be allowed to keep it?" asked his father. "I know he is to abandon all earthly possessions, but would it hurt for him to hold onto this one small reminder of home?"

Cristofano looked down at the fragile object in his hand. A monk's calling entailed severing family ties, yet as he now recalled, he himself had left the abbey briefly to visit his dying father.

"Dom Guido is now the boy's spiritual father," replied Cristofano coldly. "But I expect young Guido can be allowed to keep your chalice."

Silently he passed the cup to his nephew, who clutched it tightly with one hand while clasping his copy of St. Benedict's Rule in the other. Ardita, still fighting to hold back tears, knelt and enveloped the boy in a tight embrace.

"But Momma, it was your idea to bring me here," said Guido sharply.

Ardita pulled back abruptly, looked imploringly at Duccio, and then burst out crying.

"Goodbye, Guido. Be a good boy," said his father between his wife's wrenching sobs, patting his son on the shoulder.

Anxious to bring the scene to a close, Cristofano beckoned toward the entryway, where Valentino motioned to the parents to follow him. Gazing back mournfully at their son, they slowly withdrew. Guido stared back impassively until they were out of sight, then turned his gaze up to Cristofano. The sound of Ardita's sobbing gradually receded in the distance.

Not uttering a word, the monk led Guido into the cloister. The sun had sunk low in the sky, and the archways cast long shadows on the smooth stone walkway. As they proceeded through the deserted courtyard, Guido almost unconsciously began singing to himself in his pure, piping soprano voice.

Te Deum laudamus: te Dominum confitemur.
Te aeternum Patrem omnis terra veneratur.

Still proceeding briskly, Cristofano permitted himself to look down at the boy and nod approvingly.

Chapter Four

A NEW LIFE

Within moments, Cristofano had escorted Guido to the school and up the stairs to a long rectangular room reserved for the boys aspiring to be novices. There he placed the newcomer in the care of Brother Facio, the master of the oblates. A gentle hum of voices permeated the chamber as half a dozen other boys of various ages, all wearing black cowls like the one the abbot had placed on Guido, individually read aloud from their books. Seated on the floor around a cresset lantern hanging in the corner, the boys looked up at the new arrival.

A short, stubby monk with the usual shaved crown, Facio thanked Cristofano, who turned to leave, but then stopped and said goodbye to his nephew.

"Goodbye, uncle," responded Guido. "Or . . . should I call you Brother Cristofano?"

"That is correct," nodded his uncle stoically before taking his leave.

Still clutching the Rule of St. Benedict and the chalice his father had given him, the new oblate stood facing his new master. About average in height for his age, Guido was thin and bony, with an angular face and a thatch of light brown hair.

"What's this?" barked Brother Facio, indicating the earthenware cup in the boy's hand.

"A memento from my father," answered Guido. "My unc— Brother Cristofano told me I could keep it."

"From now on, your only earthly father is Dom Guido," said Facio sternly. "But you may keep the cup here, along with your chant book and any other books we may entrust to you in your studies." He gestured to a small wooden crate next to a rounded pillar along the wall. Guido carefully placed his chalice and St. Benedict book inside it.

"You've arrived just in time for our evening meal," continued Facio. "The oblates eat in the kitchen. Line up, everyone," he said to the other boys, ringing a small bell. "This is Guido. As our newest arrival, he is last in line."

Guido took the hint and fell into position. The oblates followed Brother Facio, marching single file down the stairs and through the cloister toward the kitchen. Suddenly the boy just ahead, a stocky redhead about Guido's age, turned and whispered, "I'm Uberto. I hate it here."

Alarmed by this unexpected confession, Guido kept walking. "I'm Guido," came his not-quite-whispered answer, prompting "I know" from Uberto and a resounding "Quiet!" from Brother Facio.

In the cluttered, torchlit kitchen, the boys took their places on wooden benches along a low table; Guido squeezed in at the end. Facio led them all in a unison prayer. A pale, flaxen-haired monk distributed ceramic bowls, cups of water, and spoons, then ladled porridge into each bowl. Guido greedily finished his portion ahead of the others and, to his surprise, received a second serving; the same was soon provided to his hungrier fellow oblates as well. *At least I'll be decently fed*, thought Guido.

A bell tinkled—another signal from Brother Facio—and the boys stood and got back into line, with Guido following the others' lead. Then it was back to the upper room at the school, where the boys knelt in prayer before unrolling their straw mats for the night. Facio handed a mat to Guido and indicated a spot on the floor.

"The boys may study after their first sleep, but if you can't read yet, you can scarcely study," Facio told Guido with a sympathetic smile. "That will change soon enough."

Guido needn't have worried. Exhausted from the unrelenting string of novel experiences, he slept straight through the first sleep into the second and would probably have slept even longer were it not for the chiming of the morning bells. His first full day as an oblate was beginning.

After a morning prayer led by Brother Facio, another monk appeared and escorted three of the older boys to the abbey church to sing Lauds, prayers offered at the first light of dawn as part of the Divine Office's daily cycle of eight liturgical rites. The rest of the oblates were allowed a short study period before going to the church for a silent low Mass. Then all the boys returned to their quarters, gathered their books, and—with Guido bringing up the rear—followed Facio to the spartan classroom on the school's ground level, where they sat stiffly at attention on wooden benches. Facio handed Guido a psalter open to the Twenty-Third Psalm and began reading aloud. At the end of each line, Facio paused for the boys to repeat it. Guido, completely ignorant of reading or writing, stammered through the psalm as best he could, trying to relate Facio's words to the letters on the page. He noticed that except for Uberto, the other boys scarcely glanced at their books.

The lesson continued with psalm after psalm. Like a nonswimmer abruptly thrown into the water for the first time, Guido flailed but tried to stay afloat as best he could. As Facio droned on, Guido began to notice that certain sounds corresponded to certain letters on the page. Concentrating as intently as possible, he soon found he could identify words that frequently recurred.

As the exercise went on, one boy accidentally read *populatio* as *copulatio*, prompting a loud guffaw and an amused poke from his nearest neighbor. Facio immediately set down his psalter, picked up a wooden rod, and repeatedly struck both boys' backs until they were wailing miserably. Uberto gave Guido a look as if to say, *You see what I mean?* In response, Guido glued his eyes to the words on the page until the seemingly interminable punishment was over. Facio then continued the lesson as if nothing had happened.

Later that first morning, Facio told the oblates to open their copies of the Rule of St. Benedict. Again the boys repeated the words read by their instructor, but now Guido was starting to learn the expectations of monastic life. Here he encountered the three vows required of all Benedictine monks: poverty (renunciation of individual property; only the most basic of meals and attire), chastity (purity of thought and body), and obedience (submission to the abbot and the rules of the monastery). Hearing Brother Facio list the three vows for the first time, Guido was mentally transported back to Talla, with the taunts of his brothers again ringing in his ears.

Guido felt like he had been in the classroom for an eternity by the time Brother Facio rang his bell and led the boys to the kitchen for a prayer of thanks. There they enjoyed the midday meal, the first of the day: carrots, a slice of bread, and a small chunk of boiled fish. Clearly the boys were expected to eat in silence, since none of the others uttered a word, so Guido said nothing as well.

Next the boys filed into the church to attend the recitation of Sext, the midday Divine Office. Afterward, the older boys worked outdoors in the garden or assisted with maintenance, while Guido and others played organized games under the direction of one of the younger monks. Then Brother Facio escorted the oblates back to the classroom, where the rotund cantor, Brother Anselmo, was waiting to begin the day's singing lessons. Facio introduced him to Guido and handed the boy a chant book, opened to the day's first hymn. Some of the words in the book were accompanied by neumes—black marks at varying heights above the text, some with squiggles indicating the direction of the next note. For a few, a horizontal line provided an approximate reference point for the neumes arrayed at different distances above it. Guido was already beginning to recognize the text's letters and even certain words, but for him the neumes were meaningless.

Anselmo stood before the boys with a monochord—a single string fixed at each end, mounted over a resonating box. Strumming the string as a whole, or stopping the string to divide it at various fractions of the full length, Anselmo was able to produce different musical pitches.

"We shall begin with *Benedicamus Domino*," announced Anselmo.

Guido looked up, uncertain, and Facio nodded to let him know the book was already open to the right page.

But once Anselmo struck the first note on the monochord and began to sing, Guido's uncertainty vanished.

"*Benedicamus Domino*," sang Anselmo, and as the boys repeated the line back, Guido confidently sang it without the slightest error. With an acute sense of pitch honed from matching the hum of his father's pottery wheel, he could accurately echo virtually any melody he heard.

"*Deo gratias*," sang Anselmo to conclude the chant, and again Guido had no difficulty in repeating words, pitch, and rhythm. His strong, clear soprano was clearly audible over the voices of the other boys.

Anselmo looked at Guido and briefly raised his eyebrows in approval before moving on to the next chant. Again and again as the afternoon wore on, Guido excelled in learning each musical phrase by rote, often in only one or two hearings. None of the other boys were as adept, and when a couple of them slipped up, the rod was again put to use.

Before wrapping up the day's session, Brother Anselmo unexpectedly asked Guido to stand. Indicating the proper page in the chant book, he asked the new oblate to sing *Benedicamus Domino* as a solo. Without even looking at the book, Guido performed the chant as if he'd been singing it all his life.

"Thank you," said Anselmo. "The lesson has ended." As the boys gathered their books, he whispered to Brother Facio, "This one will be ready to sing the Divine Office in no time."

The boys concluded the school day with an arithmetic lesson and another short scriptural recitation before returning upstairs with Brother Facio, who led them in Vespers, the liturgical prayers offered at sunset. Then at last the oblates were allowed to collapse around the room, still holding their books but not necessarily studying them. As Guido quickly learned, this short period before the evening meal was the one time of the day when the boys were free to relax and even talk among themselves.

"So how did you end up here?" asked Uberto as he sprawled beside Guido.

"I'm the third of three sons in my family, so they donated me to the monastery," answered Guido, without any sign of resentment. "One of my mother's brothers is a monk at this abbey—Brother Cristofano."

"Don't know him," muttered Uberto. "But then there must be almost a hundred monks here. Where are you from?"

"Talla."

"Where's that?"

"It's a little village in the mountains, near Arezzo."

"Arezzo! That's a long way off."

"How about you?" asked Guido. "How did you come here?"

"I'm an orphan, from Ribaldesa, a village near here. My mother died when I was born, and a few months ago my father was killed by robbers. The local priest brought me here and left me."

"Don't you like learning to read and sing?" Guido asked, recalling Uberto's unexpected confession from the night before.

"I feel like I'm in prison," whispered Uberto confidentially. "With my father I'd get to go out hunting and trapping, but here I'm cooped up day and night, and I always have to keep my mouth shut."

"I hope we can be friends," said Guido.

"At least now I'm not the new boy anymore," responded Uberto. "But do you have to show up the rest of us in the singing lessons?"

Guido turned red with embarrassment. "I wasn't trying to show anyone up," he replied. "I just love to sing. I've loved music ever since I got to hear the choir at the cathedral in Arezzo."

"It's hard on the rest of us when a new boy makes it all seem so easy," said Uberto.

"But hearing me sing the chants correctly should help you learn them," countered Guido, confident that what he was doing was right.

"I'd better study St. Benedict," said Uberto, moving closer to the lantern.

After the evening meal, the boys processed into the abbey church for the night prayer, Compline. The three older boys chanted with the professed monks while the rest of the oblates listened and prayed silently. Then what seemed like the longest day of Guido's life finally came to an end, and he slept soundly through the night. But the next morning, with the tolling of the bell tower, the whole cycle began again. As the days passed in unvarying succession, he soon mastered reading and began memorizing the psalms, canticles, and hymns. Lessons continued with the precepts of the Rule of St. Benedict, the details of the lectionary, and other Latin texts. Of particular interest to Guido was the sixth-century treatise *De institutione musica* (*The Principles of Music*) by Boethius. The boy was fascinated to learn about tones and semitones, tuning, modes, and other theoretical subjects.

Guido's musical talents continued to impress Brother Anselmo, and within a few weeks he was included with the advanced boys who sang and recited during Lauds and the Divine Office's other canonical hours throughout the day.

"I have never seen an oblate learn music as quickly as young Guido," confided Anselmo to Facio. "Perhaps someday he can be my successor as cantor."

Singing the Divine Office in the church entailed other lessons: how to process into the chancel in the proper order, how to carry a lit candle without letting it go out, how to stand with correct posture, how to attentively follow the sequence of the service. Accustomed to the tyranny of his older brothers back home, Guido quickly adapted to the monks' example and the hierarchy of seniority.

One day, the oblates were escorted to the scriptorium, a high-ceilinged, lantern-lit chamber above the library. Each boy was handed a copy of an existing book, along with a quill, an inkhorn, a knife, and a page of parchment. With several of the abbey's experienced scribes offering guidance, the boys were told to copy the letters of a book page onto the parchment. The knife came in handy for erasing mistakes and keeping the quill sharp.

As the writing lessons continued in the coming weeks, Guido enjoyed a sense of accomplishment each time he completed a sheet of manuscript. He even became comfortable adding small artistic embellishments in various colors like the ones in the original book pages.

With each passing month, Guido gradually felt more at home in his new life. After the initial onslaught of completely unfamiliar procedures, lessons, and schedules to be mastered, he came to know what to expect each day and felt increasingly confident that he could fulfill his responsibilities to the monastery.

Uberto, however, was not as quick to adapt. "I still hate it here," he grumbled one day during the free period before dinner.

"But you're almost as good a reader and singer as I am," said Guido.

"Yes, but the minute I slip up—*whap*! Out comes the rod."

"It's no worse than what I always got from my brothers."

"Well, I'm not used to it," said Uberto wearily, "and I don't think I ever will be."

Suddenly Facio tinkled his bell, signaling that the boys should line up for dinner.

"See what I mean?" whispered Uberto.

As new oblates arrived, Guido's lowly position in the hierarchy of age and seniority gradually improved. On Palm Sunday he joined the procession of boys waving palm branches and singing *Gloria, laus* around the cloister and into the church. The oblates were still excused from Matins, the nighttime liturgy between first and second sleep, but they typically participated in the other seven hours of the Divine Office and chanted at daily Masses. Throughout the day, the ringing of the tower bells was their signal to form a procession and assemble with the abbey's monks in the chancel.

Month followed month, and soon year followed year. Each morning the boys arose before dawn, washed their faces and hands, and were led by Brother Facio to the church, where—amid the mosaics of the saints and bejeweled statues of Jesus and the Virgin Mary—they participated in the office of Lauds. Next came the early morning and midmorning rites—Prime around six o'clock and Terce around nine o'clock, both followed by Mass. Sext was offered at noon, and None at midafternoon. Vespers, the evening prayer, coincided with the lighting of lamps; Compline, or night prayer, was offered before bedtime. The boys were at the church performing in services almost six hours a day, reciting and singing psalms and prayers of the divine liturgy.

Between services they were at the school, learning to imitate the reading and writing of Brother Facio and the chanting of Brother Anselmo. Any "free" time was devoted to individual or group practice.

A substantial proportion of the oblates' day was spent singing. As the quickest study, Guido was often entrusted with vocal solos, his clear, piping voice soaring to the rafters of the church's reverberant nave. Even jealous boys like Uberto could not help appreciating the beauty and conviction of his singing.

In Guido's third year at Pomposa, one of the older monks fell ill and died. Although Guido felt somewhat guilty, given the occasion, he could not help enjoying his participation in the special pomp of the Requiem Mass. He got to carry a candle in the procession around the cloister to the church, and Brother Anselmo assigned him to sing a solo as part of the service. So striking was his performance that afterward, the abbot asked the cantor, "Who was the boy soprano who sang so beautifully?"

"Ah, Lord Abbot," replied Anselmo, "it is interesting that you ask."

"Why is that?"

Smiling reverentially, Anselmo answered, "His name is the same as yours."

It was only then that the abbot belatedly remembered the boy's oblation ceremony—and the "Guido" chalice.

One early morning, during Lauds, Guido's voice cracked. As the day's canonical hours wore on, he found it harder and harder to sing in his accustomed range. After Vespers, he approached the cantor.

"I'm sorry, Brother Anselmo. I don't know what's wrong with my voice today."

"Don't worry, Guido. This day arrives for every boy singer. Your voice is changing. Soon you'll sing with the men of the monastery instead of with the boys."

Guido then remembered that several of his fellow oblates had already made this vocal transition. Somehow he had imagined that his own "promotion" would be far in the future.

"But this is not just about your singing," continued the monk. "When your voice changes, that means your days as an oblate are ending. You are ready to become a novice."

Guido felt a pang of concern as he contemplated the impending change in his now-familiar routine. "How do you know my mind and my spirit are as ready as my body?" he dared to ask.

Anselmo rolled his eyes. "What a question! I'm sure you are ready. I will notify the abbot."

The next afternoon, in the oblates' room before the evening meal, Guido reported these developments to Uberto. Slower to mature than his contemporary, Uberto was still singing comfortably in the treble register.

"Soon I'll be sleeping in the dormitory," said Guido gloomily. "But you'll be following me there soon."

"And you're about to get the top of your head shaved," laughed Uberto.

Once again, Guido remembered the taunts of his brothers—especially the day they went for his scalp with the shears.

Guido's promotion to novice came soon enough. After the morning Mass following the office of Terce, the monks customarily assembled in the chapter house for their daily meeting, with the oblates sitting silently at the rear. The boys always tried to look attentive as the abbot led an opening prayer, read from the Rule of St. Benedict, and guided a discussion of various articles of business. On this occasion, at the appropriate time, Brother Facio came forward with Guido and presented him to the abbot as a candidate for the novitiate.

"Ah, the other Guido," nodded the abbot.

The lad stood nervously as Brother Facio was questioned about Guido's progress and attitude. This was a formality for the community's benefit, since Guido's spiritual and moral growth had been carefully appraised beforehand by Cristofano, Facio, and the abbot. Next, the abbot signaled for the decision of the professed monks, whose vote would determine whether Guido should be accepted into the community. The imposing Prior Pangratio—the abbey's second in command—stepped forward and announced their decision to invite Guido into the novitiate.

Before returning to the day's routine after the meeting, the other oblates offered their congratulations, although Uberto remained silent and distant. Guido found this puzzling but had no opportunity to speak with him.

That evening at Vespers, Guido's novitiate year officially began with the rite of monastic initiation. He was given a tunic to wear like the other novices and knelt to receive the "monastic crown" from Prior Pangratio, who approached with a razor and a bowl of water. Performing the traditional rite of tonsure, the prior shaved the top of Guido's head with a practiced hand.

So this is what it feels like, thought Guido as the blade grazed his scalp. *At least the first time is probably the hardest.*

Recalling the inscription on Guido's earthenware chalice, the abbot decided not to give the potter's son a new name. "In Latin, Guido means 'guide,'" he said. "May you guide others to God by your prayers and your work."

From that day forward, the new novice was called Brother Guido.

At last he was allowed to stand, and the abbot blessed him, made the sign of the cross, and led the monks in prayer. For better or worse, Guido began to feel the truth of what Cristofano had said on the day of his oblation. However exalted and remote the abbot seemed to be, Dom Guido had now become young Guido's spiritual father.

At the conclusion of the chapter meeting, Guido was placed in the care of Brother Nicolo, the tall, salt-and-pepper-haired monk who was master of the novices. For each new novice, Nicolo assigned an older monk as *custos animi*—guardian of the soul—and he had asked Cristofano to serve in that capacity. *Perhaps now I'll get to know my uncle a little better*, thought Guido, wary of Cristofano's typical remoteness.

As Nicolo started to lead him toward the dormitory, Guido stopped in panic.

"What is it?" asked Nicolo.

"I was allowed to keep one possession, a chalice made by my father," said Guido with unexpected boldness. "May I retrieve it from the oblates' room?"

Surprised by the request, Nicolo answered, "I will accompany you," and together they climbed the stairs of the school. The chalice was still resting in the wooden crate against the wall, just as Guido had left it on his first day at the abbey.

"Thank you," said Guido after retrieving the treasured article and handing it to Nicolo for safekeeping. "I am ready now."

As they proceeded through the cloister toward the dormitory, the accustomed silence was interrupted by shouting, and monks could be seen running in all directions. Never in all his time at Pomposa had Guido seen anything like it.

"What has happened?" Nicolo asked an agitated monk who was racing toward the entrance.

"One of the oblates has run away!" came the answer. "Uberto is gone!"

Guido felt a sudden chill pass through his entire body. He stood immobilized until Nicolo seized his hand and quickly ushered him toward the dormitory. Climbing the dark stairs to the novices' quarters, he felt that, in their own very different ways, both he and Uberto were plunging into the unknown.

Chapter Five

FROM NOVICE TO MONK

As a novice under the tutelage of Brother Nicolo, Guido began learning a new litany of rituals. Many were related to deportment: how and when to bow to superiors, when and where to sit and stand. Now that he wore a black tunic and scapular rather than the simple cowl of the oblates, he also received discreet instruction in how to dress and undress. He began to learn how the hierarchy of position, age, and seniority dictated seating arrangements in the church, the refectory, and chapter meetings. Meanwhile, the novices' musical training for singing the chants of the Divine Office continued under Brother Anselmo, but now in the chapter house. Brother Cristofano assured Guido that he was available to answer any questions, but otherwise he remained uninvolved in the novice's training.

The biggest difference between oblation and the novitiate was a deepening of spiritual life. Guido entered a period of intense study, prayer, and reflection that tested his suitability for a lifetime in the monastery. He was challenged to understand and articulate his divine vocation and to grow in his relationship with God. Instead of merely learning to read the sacred scripture, the Rule of St. Benedict, and the lives of the saints, he was now expected to internalize their lessons.

On a practical level, this included learning to confess and ask pardon for faults. Oblates relied on their master's rod for making them aware of infractions, but novices were expected to monitor their own behavior and to abase themselves whenever they fell short. Guido took his vocation so seriously that his infractions were mercifully rare, at least in action. But in thought, he sometimes found himself questioning the status quo, and then wondering if he had erred by doing so. Often, after the usual long morning without food, the novices were required to sit silently in the kitchen and watch the midday meal being prepared. "I guess this is supposed to teach us self-control," he once muttered impatiently to himself—a remark that no one overheard, but later he wondered if it called for a confession.

The novices joined the full-fledged monks in the refectory for both of the daily meals, maintaining total silence as the abbot read from the Rule of St. Benedict while the food was served. Gradually Guido began to learn the abbey's unofficial sign language—such as forming a circle with the thumbs and index fingers of both hands to communicate "please pass the bread," since the loaves were round.

Each day Guido now sang and recited prayers for all eight canonical hours of the Divine Office, even Matins—the long nighttime service beginning well before dawn. The rest of his routine included daily spiritual instruction from Brother Nicolo, the ever-continuing music training with Brother Anselmo in the chapter house, and, for his first time at Pomposa, manual labor in the kitchen and gardens. Now that he was getting less sleep because of Matins, he was always completely exhausted by the time he was allowed to unroll his mat and blanket on the floor of the novices' chamber.

Guido's greatest trial was following the Benedictine requirement of perpetual humility. He could easily be humble about his skill at planting seeds in the garden, washing dishes in the kitchen, or even copying manuscripts in the scriptorium. But although he had shifted to a lower vocal register as a baritone, he still knew that he sang beautifully and accurately and that he learned music much more quickly than any of the other novices, or even most of the monks.

In sessions learning melodies from the chant book with Brother Anselmo at the chapter house, whenever a singer standing near him made an error, Guido's natural inclination was to point out the mistake and demonstrate how to sing the phrase correctly. And each time he did this, he was forced to lie prostrate on the ground at Brother Anselmo's feet and confess his sin. Eventually he learned to merely give erring singers a sharp glance of disapproval, prompting them to confess their own mistakes so that they were the ones falling to the floor. Anselmo sometimes noticed Guido's subtle signals but at least considered this behavior an improvement.

And yet music was also Guido's one sure pathway to spirituality. Reading about God in the Bible seemed abstract, and when asked to describe his devotion to the Church, he fell back on repeating familiar homilies without any real depth of feeling. But when he was singing, whether as a soloist or with the rest of the choir, Guido genuinely felt closer to heaven. The music always seemed to purify his soul and lift it to a higher plane.

One late night, after Matins, Brother Anselmo took Guido aside.

"I would tell you that you sang beautifully at Matins," said the monk, "but I don't want to encourage an unseemly sense of superiority."

"I sing only for the glory of God," responded Guido, knowing what Anselmo wanted to hear.

"I am probably about twenty years older than you," Anselmo went on, "and I hope to train the singers here for many more years to come. But when I find I can no longer continue, I already know who will be the monk most qualified to succeed me as cantor."

Guido's eyes opened wide.

"I tell you this not to make you less humble," Anselmo continued, "but to charge you with a great spiritual goal. You must learn to practice your talents meekly, always aware that those talents are not of your own making, but a gift from God."

"But I'm the one who makes the effort to practice and learn all the music, even if God gave me the talent," said Guido with inappropriate candor.

"Guido!" barked Anselmo with an all-too-familiar look.

Painfully aware that he had again spoken his mind too freely, Guido prostrated himself on the floor of the church. "I have committed the sin of arrogance. I beg the Lord's forgiveness."

Lifting the novice to his feet, the cantor sighed and said, "I see that you still have much progress to make."

As the year of his novitiate began drawing to a close, Guido underwent frequent interrogations from Brother Nicolo to determine the depth of his spiritual growth. Mentally, he was torn between guilt that he felt less close to God than he should and a growing discomfort with the religious regimentation he was expected to accept with humility. But he had mastered St. Benedict's Rule, he knew the right answers to Nicolo's questions, and he had been obliged to prostrate himself at Brother Anselmo's feet with steadily decreasing frequency.

As the appointed day approached, Guido worked tirelessly to draw up his required petition to the abbot. Unlike some newly arrived novices who had not yet learned to write, he wrote his appeal himself and signed his name just as it appeared on the chalice from his father. Gazing at the fragile little vessel, he gravely contemplated how to make it part of the ceremony.

As Mass was about to begin on the morning marking the end of his novitiate year, Guido took his place at the back of the church, his petition in hand. By now grown to almost his full adult height (taller than Anselmo, shorter than Nicolo), he was still thin, but his frame had filled out enough that it was no longer the jumble of jagged edges that had first appeared at Pomposa. Even his still-angular face now bore traces of resemblance to his comely mother. Standing up straight, his weight evenly placed on both feet, he was determined to demonstrate that he had mastered all his lessons, including deportment.

At the appropriate time during the service, while Brother Anselmo led the monks in chanting, Guido was escorted to the altar by Brother Nicolo as master of novices, Brother Facio as master of oblates, Brother Cristofano as nominal guardian of his soul, and Brother Valentino, the hosteler who had first welcomed him and his parents to Pomposa.

Before Dom Guido and the entire community, Guido read his petition aloud. He then promised to obey the Rule of St. Benedict and pledged his perpetual steadfastness to a new life of poverty, chastity, and obedience to God. As an indication of acceptance, the abbot removed Guido's novice cowl and offered him his new habit, the black hooded scapular.

Having had plenty of practice, Guido solemnly prostrated himself on the church floor while all present recited the Litany of the Saints, invoking the saints' help in the fulfillment of Guido's vocation. He was then raised up by the abbot, who gave his blessing: "*In nomine Patris, et Filii, et Spiritus Sancti.*"

"As evidence of your devotion, Brother Guido," continued the abbot, "I understand you have something of value that you would like to offer up to God?"

Taking his father's cherished earthenware cup from Brother Nicolo, who had been holding it in the folds of his scapular, Guido replied, "Lord Abbot, I relinquish this chalice, which my father, a potter, made with his own hands on the day of my birth. No possession could be dearer to me, but I freely surrender it as a sign of my consecration to God."

Despite the solemnity of the occasion, a brief murmur

rippled through the assembled monks, who were accustomed to novices making less personal offerings.

Dom Guido, smiling as he saw his own name on the side of the chalice, turned toward the chancel's mounted crucifix and lifted the cup high above his head with both hands, intoning his blessings on the gift. He started to hand the chalice to Prior Pangratio, but then unexpectedly kept it, turning to face the new monk.

"You have sacrificed an object of great significance in your life. This renunciation is ample proof of your devotion."

Guido bowed his head reverently, but the abbot continued.

"And so you may keep the chalice. Just as God spared Isaac's life after Abraham proved that he was willing to sacrifice his son, I will spare you the sacrifice of this memento. Treasure it as a token of your dedication to God."

As the abbot placed Guido's hands around the fragile little cup, the potter's son burst into tears. For the first time, he felt a genuine connection to his spiritual father.

Being the newest in the monks' seniority, Guido now slept on a pallet at the coldest end of the dormitory's long central room. As Brother Nicolo had instructed him to expect, he wore his new monastic cassock morning, noon, and night for three days, maintaining complete silence—his greatest challenge—for the entire period. And also as expected, he was accompanied everywhere by a guardian to make sure he faithfully followed all the rules of the abbey. Like Nicolo in selecting Guido's guardian of the soul, the abbot had assigned Cristofano to fulfill this function. But his uncle was no less aloof than before, giving no sign for the entire three days that Guido was anything but just another new monk admitted to the monastery. Even at the close of the third day, although Guido searched Cristofano's face for some sign of familiarity, the older monk remained completely impassive, all the way through the moment when he presented his nephew to Prior Pangratio.

Managing the housekeeping chores for this transition, the prior handed Guido a small wooden crate containing a writing tablet and stylus, a wooden comb, needles and thread, and a knife. For Guido, this would also be the receptacle for the chalice he had been allowed to keep.

As Guido returned to the dormitory—permitted to walk through the cloister alone for the first time since he arrived at Pomposa at age ten—he thought, *So at last I am a monk. I have fulfilled my parents' wishes. I will serve God here the rest of my days, and here will I breathe my last.* With determination if not deep devotion, he threw himself into his new routine. And every day when the monks rehearsed with Brother Anselmo, any time a fellow singer made a mistake, Guido kept quiet—even if he had to bite his lip.

Chapter Six

A NEW ARRIVAL

Guido quickly settled into the monastery's unvarying routine. Each day he dressed in his black woolen tunic and hooded scapular. Once a week he would line up with the other monks for the ritual head shaving so that their scalps stayed bald and their tonsures remained neat and trim. Four times a year, the monks were allowed to bathe individually in cold water. Once a year, they went to the infirmary for ritual bleeding, to rid the body of toxins. At Christmas, each monk was given a new cassock and robe.

The abbey's daily activities were adjusted with the cycle of the seasons as sunrise and sunset shifted, but the order of the day was largely predictable. The monks awoke a few hours before dawn for the nighttime office of Matins, processing down the dormitory's back stairs directly to the chapel to avoid going out into the open air of the cloister. They then washed up and occupied themselves in silent activity—praying, reading, mending, or copying a manuscript in the scriptorium. After the dawn office of Lauds, Brother Anselmo would rehearse the monks in the chapter house on the hymns, songs, and canticles to be sung in the day's remaining services. Prime, the early morning office, was followed by morning Mass. With the conclusion of that service, the monks would return to the chapter house for the daily meeting, where abbey business was discussed; Guido was pleased to discover that here, at least, the free expression of opinions was tolerated.

Terce, the midmorning office, was followed by work in the gardens, fields, kitchen, or scriptorium, or at the monastery gate distributing food to the poor and hungry who came to the abbey for help. Next came midday Mass and the midday meal, where the only speaking was the abbot's readings from the Rule of St. Benedict. Work continued following the afternoon's canonical hours—Sext at midday and None at midafternoon. After the evening meal came the office of Vespers and the lighting of lamps. A final work period preceded Compline, the night office, before the monks retired to sleep on their straw mats in the dormitory. And then the cycle began again as the monks woke up for Matins; one brother always poked around with a lamp to make sure no one was still sleeping.

Like all of medieval Europe, Guido believed what he had been taught to believe, all the more easily because of his enforced isolation from the outside world. If his convictions were less fervent than those of the abbey's most devoted monks, they were nevertheless untainted by doubt.

In rehearsing the chants with Brother Anselmo, Guido still occasionally gave his erring brothers a reproving look, but for the most part he had disciplined himself to let the other monks confess musical mistakes on their own. His own admissions of fault were primarily a consequence of speaking out too freely at chapter meetings. Although differing viewpoints were encouraged, he soon learned that any time he suggested a more efficient procedure for a haphazardly organized monastic activity, the abbot invariably stuck with the tried and true.

And so the years went by, with Guido reasonably content to expect that nothing in his life would ever change. Until one day when he was in his mid-twenties, something happened that would change everything.

After a chapter meeting on a sunny fall day, Guido was approached by Brother Nicolo, still the master of the novices.

"Brother Guido, there's someone I'd like you to meet."

"Yes?" answered Guido respectfully.

"We have a new novice named Michael. He's nineteen years old, and he's the youngest of three brothers, just like you. I would like you to be his *custos animi*—his guardian of the soul."

"I am happy to serve in any way I can," said Guido, recalling Cristofano's minimal involvement in his own novitiate.

Leading Guido toward the kitchen, where the novices were learning to assist in preparing meals, Nicolo provided additional background.

"Michael is of noble parentage, so he has been well educated—he's already fluent in reading and writing," said Nicolo. "He has a great love of learning, and since there are two brothers ahead of him in the line of inheritance, and he's not inclined to join the army, he has come here in hopes of pursuing a scholarly life."

"I hope he also loves hoeing and weeding," remarked Guido, who was not especially enamored of the abbey's requirement for outdoor labor.

"Ah, here he is," said Nicolo, gesturing to Michael as they entered the kitchen.

Physical appearance carried no advantage in the world of the abbey, but even as he stood clustered among the other novices amid pots and pans, Michael made a striking impression. Wearing an ordinary black cowl, with his head already tonsured, he had a face that could only be described—at least in this religious setting—as angelic. And the ring of shimmering blonde hair around his shaved scalp was his halo. Judging from the way he held his tall, graceful frame, no training in deportment would be necessary.

Immediately warming to the new novice as they were introduced, Guido bowed in welcome. Michael's broad and sincere smile of greeting instantly showed that their sympathetic understanding was mutual. For reasons mysterious to them both, the two felt an instant bond.

"Brother Guido has agreed to assist me in your monastic training," said Nicolo to Michael.

"I would be honored," the novice replied.

Bowing again to the new arrival, Guido said, "I look forward to being of service."

~

Preoccupied with the less educated novices, Brother Nicolo largely left Michael's training to Guido, whose involvement as guardian of the soul was thus much greater than his own guardian's had been. Whether copying manuscripts in the scriptorium, studying ecclesiastical doctrine in the cloister, or harvesting vegetables in the garden, Guido and Michael enjoyed a comfortable, friendly give-and-take that neither had ever previously experienced.

Proceeding from the refectory to the church for Vespers when the bell sounded after an evening meal, Michael confided, "You know, I wasn't sure I was going to like it here, but you've made me feel part of the abbey from the very beginning."

"I'm glad you believe it was the right decision," said Guido.

"It was all my family's idea."

"For me too!" said Guido. "Except I was too young to even know what I was getting into."

"Do you want to know the real reason they sent me here?"

"I thought you wanted to live a scholarly life."

"I do, yes. But what forced the decision was when . . . ." Michael hesitated.

"What happened?" asked Guido with concern, sensing that a confidence was about to be shared. He was not mistaken.

"I had a third cousin, a very beautiful girl, who was betrothed to the son of a count. But we . . . the two of us . . . well, before long, she was with child. Because of me."

Guido glimpsed a world of which he was entirely ignorant.

"It was a big family scandal. So she had to become a nun, and I had to become a monk," Michael continued with a wry smile.

"And the child?" asked Guido.

"My parents were going to raise her as their own, but she died of the fever just before I came here."

"Did you . . . love this woman?" asked Guido delicately.

"I . . . desired her," answered Michael. "I'm not sure we were in love."

"And you're comfortable now taking a vow of chastity?"

"If you can do it, I guess I can too," said Michael, playfully jabbing Guido in the ribs.

Michael progressed rapidly in his novitiate training in all areas but one. Whenever Brother Anselmo was teaching the novices to sing the sacred chants, Michael was always the slowest to catch on. Although he possessed a beautiful singing voice, he seemed to spend the majority of the practice sessions prostrate on the floor, confessing his mistakes.

Later, with Guido, Michael bewailed his musical ineptitude.

"I just can't seem to get it," he moaned. "Brother Anselmo sings a phrase, and everyone else sings it back, but when I sing it back, I never sing it right."

"Can't you follow the neumes in the chant book? They're the little black dots at different heights above the words, showing how high or low the notes are."

"A lot of the chants don't even have any neumes. And for the ones that do, they only work as a reminder once you've already learned how the chant goes," protested Michael. "They're no help in learning something you don't already know."

As someone who learned new music with little difficulty, Guido found it hard to put himself in the place of anyone lacking his special talents. But he realized that Michael's observation was all too accurate.

"The more you hear the hymns and psalms, the sooner they'll all start to sink in," said Guido, hoping his optimism was justified.

"You'd better be right," said Michael. "Otherwise I might as well stay sprawled on the floor for every rehearsal."

From then on, whenever an opportunity arose, Guido would sing a chant melody to Michael and listen as he tried to replicate it. But it was a trial-and-error process, and Michael's musical progress continued to stall. Once, after Mass, Guido even had the temerity to ask Brother Anselmo if he could be of any help with Michael.

"He'll catch on eventually," said Anselmo, waving him off. "Everyone does, sooner or later."

But will his knees give out from always falling to the floor? thought Guido.

As the day approached when Michael was to take his monastic vows, Guido helped him craft his petition. Deciding on a possession to sacrifice was easy; Michael's family had given him a valuable book on the lives of the martyrs that he intended to donate to the abbey's library.

"How has your spirituality deepened since you came here?" asked Guido, making sure not to neglect the most important aspect of a novice's training. After all, unlike Guido, Michael was not likely to find spiritual fulfillment in singing.

Michael pondered for a moment before responding. "You have taught me to experience the communion of souls—an earthly foretaste of the saints' communion in heaven," he said thoughtfully. "Through you, I have come to understand the blessed friendship of David and Jonathan, and of Jesus and his disciple John. Because of you, I truly know what it is to love thy neighbor as thyself."

Guido returned Michael's intense gaze. "You have taught me as well," he said at last. "Your struggles with singing have helped me learn patience and kindness. I feel God working through you to refine my heart."

Michael smiled. "I only hope God will work through you to refine my singing."

The morning of Michael's investiture as a monk, Guido went through his routines as usual. But he was acutely conscious that a special era was about to end. As the monk entrusted by Brother Nicolo with supervising Michael's training, Guido had indeed enjoyed a communion of kindred spirits unlike anything he had ever experienced. Once Michael was a monk, there would be no further need for out-of-the-ordinary interaction, and in fact St. Benedict had specifically warned against brother joining brother at "unsuitable times." Guido knew that a different monk had been named to serve as Michael's guardian for the traditional three days of initial supervision. He hoped their friendship could survive this transition without provoking animosity or suspicion.

Only a few hours later, the monks assembled in the church for Mass. At the appointed time during the service, with Guido and Brother Nicolo close at hand, Michael proceeded to the altar and—as he had done so many times before when confessing musical faults—prostrated himself on the floor. Like every monk accepted at Pomposa, he offered a prayer, promised to obey the Rule of St. Benedict, and made the traditional pledges of stead-fastness and obedience. The rite continued as the abbot raised him to his feet, accepted his petition, exchanged his novice's cowl for a monk's cassock, and finished with the sign of the cross. The presentation of the book for the monastery's library completed the ceremony. Michael was now a monk.

It was only after the midday meal a few days later that Guido had a brief opportunity to speak with his friend.

"Congratulations, and welcome to the brotherhood," said Guido formally, conscious that his duties as guardian of Michael's soul had come to an end.

"Thanks to you!" exclaimed Michael, as if nothing at all had changed. "I couldn't have done it without you."

"Oh, yes, you could've," said Guido with a spontaneous smile. "But I'm glad I could help."

"And I'm not done needing your help," said Michael.

"I'm always available to be of service," said Guido, not sure what Michael meant.

"You have to keep helping me with my singing!" said Michael. "For me, trying to learn a new chant is like trying to learn a foreign language. It seems as though every other note I sing is wrong."

"You just need more practice," said Guido, trying to sound encouraging.

But as he reflected on the conversation in the days ahead, he wondered if there was anything more he could do to help his friend.

Chapter Seven

A BREAKTHROUGH

The monks were all gathered in the chapter house as usual for their morning rehearsal of the day's service music. "We will begin by reviewing *Ubi caritas*," Brother Anselmo announced. Standing before them with the monochord, he ascertained where to stop the string to produce the correct first pitch, then plucked it vigorously. The monks collectively hummed the note.

"*Ubi caritas est vera*," sang Anselmo.

"*Ubi caritas est vera*," repeated the cassocked chorus in unison.

"*Deus ibi est*," continued Anselmo.

"*Deus ibi est*," came the unison echo.

The following phrases repeated the same melody as the first two and so were also echoed successfully: "*Congregavit nos in unum Christi amor. Exultemus, et in ipso iucundemur.*" But then Anselmo sang the next phrase, which started on the same note but continued with an entirely different melody: "*Timeamus, et amemus Deum vivum.*"

"*Timeamus, et amemus Deum vivum*," repeated the monks,

but this time not entirely in unison. A few stray wrong notes near the end were clearly audible.

Brother Michael threw himself to the floor. "I freely confess my error," he said wearily. "May I be forgiven for my faults."

Brother Anselmo snapped. "Brother Michael, what is wrong with you? We've gone over this time and again, and you never get it right!"

Much as they tried to control their reactions, the assembled monks let out an audible gasp at this unaccustomed break in decorum.

Brother Anselmo turned away from the choir, clasped his hands behind his back, and, with head bowed, took a few steps toward the rear of the room. When he turned again to face the assembled monks, he fell to his knees.

"I have sinned, and I beg forgiveness for my fault," he said before prostrating himself on the floor. "I should not lose my temper."

After a few moments he stood and resumed the rehearsal. Several more confessions of error ensued as the session wore on; not all of them were by Brother Michael, but he was by far the most frequent offender.

As Guido gazed down at the chant book, he understood Michael's plight. The neumes—the little black dots above the words—were just there to jog your memory once you'd learned the melody. They didn't tell you what notes to sing if you didn't know them already.

The next day, in the abbey's well-appointed library, he asked the reverend librarian if the abbey owned any chant collections with more precise musical notation.

"I don't know of any chant books with a different system," came the answer, "but I think we have a copy of a work suggesting another approach."

Searching the shelves, the librarian located the anonymous *Musica enchiriadis*, a widely circulated treatise from the preceding century, and opened it to an explanatory page. The manuscript used four shapes, rotated in different directions, to represent the notes of the scale—the seven consecutive tones that formed the basis of the chant melodies.

"I can see why this never caught on," said Guido impatiently. "It's too confusing. The symbols are too hard to tell apart."

"I've heard that the Greek Church uses symbols for each syllable—one to indicate staying on the same pitch as the note before, one that means to go up a step, one for going up two steps, another for down a step, and so on," said the librarian. "But there would be so many different symbols to memorize."

"And if you get off pitch, there's no way to get back on," agreed Guido.

Thanking the librarian cordially as he left, Guido continued to wonder if there might be a better approach.

That afternoon, he and Michael were both assigned to work in the garden. The sun was hot, but a cool breeze ruffled the leaves. As their progress took them further and further from the outbuildings, and since for the moment no one else was around to observe them, Michael surreptitiously approached Guido and spoke.

"I don't know how much longer I can stand the humiliation," moaned Michael. "And now I'm even leading Brother Anselmo into sin. If I keep struggling like this, I don't know . . . I may even have to renounce my vows and leave the monastery."

"Michael, no!" exclaimed Guido impulsively—forgetting the Benedictine admonition to "listen." More formally, he continued, "Your vows are sacred."

"Maybe I'm just not cut out to be a monk after all," said Michael. "At least not a singing monk."

"But what would you do out in the world?" asked Guido, hoping to put a quick end to this train of thought.

"I could hire myself out as a traveling scribe, notating letters and documents for people who can't read or write," answered Michael.

Guido realized with a shock that apparently his friend had already given the possibility some thought.

"Don't talk of such things," said Guido. "Let's try the chant that Brother Anselmo started with today."

Patiently, Guido intoned each phrase of *Ubi caritas* and listened carefully as Michael tried to repeat after him. Each time Michael made an error, Guido good-naturedly corrected it.

"At least out here I don't have to fall to the ground every time I make a mistake," laughed Michael.

Trying to find something to compliment in his protégé's efforts, Guido said, "You have a beautiful voice. And you're very good at the rhythm. You always sing each syllable with the correct duration."

"That's the easy part," said Michael. "The rhythm is all about the words—just like speaking. But the pitches are another story."

"We will find a way," said Guido, more determined than ever to figure out something that would help his friend.

A few days later, while copying a chant book in the scriptorium, Guido thought back to the system described in the treatise at the library. *After all*, he reasoned, *there are only seven different notes in the scale—A, B, C, D, E, F, and G, which then repeat at each next higher octave. And every chant we sing uses only those seven scale tones—even if the pitches' organization may vary from chant to chant, depending on which form of the scale is used.*

A new thought came to him. *What if each of the seven notes was represented by a neume of a different ink color?*

Suddenly inspired, Guido took a scrap piece of parchment and wrote out the words of the first stanza of *Ubi caritas*, leaving extra space for all the melismas—syllables extending across multiple notes. Then, singing the chant quietly, he figured out which of the scale tones matched each of the notes of the melody. From lowest to highest, he indicated them using a rainbow of colors: red, blue, green, purple, orange, brown, and black. So now in Guido's makeshift manuscript, above the words was a string of colored neumes instead of the variously but vaguely positioned black dots of the standard chant book.

"Try this," said Guido triumphantly the next time he and Michael found themselves working together in the garden. First

Guido sang the seven tones of the scale, from lowest to highest, pausing to identify each note's unique color. After Michael echoed this rendition, Guido handed him the parchment.

Michael did well enough in the opening lines, because by now he had already learned those phrases. But as the ensuing lines became less and less familiar, he stumbled repeatedly. "Wait, which note is green?" he stopped to ask before trying to plow ahead. "It's hard to tell purple from black," he lamented a phrase later. Finally he stopped completely.

"It doesn't work," sighed Michael in exasperation. "I still don't know how to get from one note to the next."

"You don't *need* to know how to get from one note to the next," retorted Guido impatiently. "All you have to do is relate every note to a fixed tone in the scale."

Michael gamely tried to continue, but with no better luck. At last he gave up and tossed the parchment into the air.

"I'm sorry, Guido. Thanks for trying," Michael exclaimed. Then quickly trying to defuse the situation, he added, "It might work for someone else, but I'm just too hopeless." With that he retreated despondently to the other side of the garden.

Thinking over the unfortunate results of this experiment, Guido realized the weakness of his color scheme. There was no rhyme or reason about which color followed which in the progression up the scale. So someone like Michael first had to look at each neume and then figure out which scale tone its color represented before he could finally sing the syllable on that scale tone. The method was too complicated for anyone trying to sing a chant at a normal pace.

Guido had hit upon a concept that he would not perfect until years later: the idea of giving each scale step a fixed identity. But for now he went back to the drawing board.

When he was next at work in the scriptorium, Guido grabbed a new scrap of parchment and again wrote out the words of *Ubi caritas*, with plenty of space for extra notes on the melismatic syllables. Remembering that some chants were written with the neumes at various heights above a horizontal line, he drew a straight line across the page from beginning to end of the first line of text.

What if this line represents one fixed note of the scale? he wondered. *And if I draw a neume so that it rests directly on the line—half above and half below—it would mean to sing that specific pitch?*

Since *Ubi caritas* began with the same pitch (F) on both syllables of "*U-bi*," it seemed logical to place that pitch on the line. Letting his mind continue to wander, Guido reflected that the next note in the melody was G, a step above F, to begin the syllable "*ca-*." He realized that if his horizontal line represented one specific pitch, then a neume directly above the line, but barely touching it, could be the next highest note of the scale. If a neume on the line was F, a neume riding on top of the line would be G. So above the appropriate words, Guido entered neumes for the chant's first three pitches—two F's on the line and a G immediately above it.

Surveying his work so far, Guido saw that, whatever the mysteries of the melody's other pitches, the notes for "*U-bi ca-*" were now indicated exactly, without any confusion or ambiguity.

Then came another moment of revelation. *Wait*, he thought. *If a neume immediately above the line stands for the next step higher than the line, then a neume immediately* below *the line can stand for the next step lower than the line.*

The trouble with that idea was that in *Ubi caritas*, the next pitch—continuing the syllable *"ca-"*—was A, another step higher. There was only one solution, though he reached the conclusion grudgingly. He had to tear up this page and start over.

Searching around the scriptorium until he found yet another discarded scrap of parchment, Guido wrote out just the first phrase of the *Ubi caritas* text with appropriate spacing, then again added the horizontal line above the words. But this time, for the initial pitch on *"U-bi,"* he carefully inscribed the neumes just below—but touching—the horizontal line. Then he added neumes directly onto the line for the next higher note and neumes immediately above the line for the next higher pitch beyond that. Since the words *Ubi caritas* used only those three pitches, he had now notated the melody for those words with perfect accuracy!

Let's see what Michael thinks of this, thought Guido, stuffing the parchment into a pocket of his tunic. During a few unstructured moments after the next day's unusually brief chapter meeting, he drew Michael out into the open area of the cloister.

"Try this," said Guido, explaining what the positioning of the neumes meant relative to the horizontal line. And indeed, once Michael understood the system, he sang the words "Ubi caritas" with complete confidence. But he stopped before continuing to the next word. "Now what do I do when the next note goes higher?"

"You're right, of course," conceded Guido, pondering the challenge. "I guess this is just a start to solving the problem."

"Say," said Michael brightly, "if one horizontal line is good, how about adding another one?"

Grabbing the page from him, Guido exclaimed excitedly, "And the lines would need to be close enough together so that the top of the note immediately above *this* line would just barely touch the new line that's directly above it!"

Bells began ringing to summon them to the church for Terce, so Guido again pocketed his manuscript. But he could barely wait to return to the scriptorium that afternoon.

Setting out the page on his writing desk, Guido carefully added a new horizontal line so it barely abutted the top of the neumes that he had positioned just above the line below. When he had finished, he noticed that those notes now occupied a clear-cut space between the two lines. So pitches could be specified by positioning them either on a line, or within a space.

And that's when the real "eureka" moment arrived. If a second line was good, why not a third and fourth line above those? The resulting grid would create enough lines and spaces to represent every note of the scale, even with room to spare for chants that extended up to the octave above the lowest note.

Quickly adding the additional lines, Guido filled in neumes for the first few phrases of *Ubi caritas* in their entirety. Each space or line signified a step of the scale; each pitch of the chant's initial melody was now notated precisely, without any chance of confusion.

Working his way through the strophe, however, Guido encountered a new obstacle in the phrase where Michael's error had drawn Brother Anselmo's ire. The melody for the word *amemus*—and, later, for *diligamus*—extended downward well below the chant's first note, the note he had placed just below the lowest line. And the way he had situated the pitches on the four-line grid, this particular chant melody didn't go high enough to ever utilize the two top lines or two top spaces. Once again, he was forced to start over, this time arranging the melody on the grid so the lowest pitch (C) fell on the space below the lowest line. It was all a matter of deciding which scale notes fell where on this grid of lines—or, as Guido eventually termed it, the staff.

But just because he knew which pitch belonged where, how would Michael know? After a few minutes, he found an easy solution: a signal to indicate which pitch was represented by a specific staff line. A red staff line could stand for the note F and a yellow line for the note C. Or he could write the note-name letter itself on the appropriate line at the beginning of the chant (the precursor to latter-day clef symbols)—for *Ubi caritas*, placing a C on the uppermost of the four horizontal lines. Then the other notes could easily be determined by their line or space position relative to those landmarks.

This time carefully rolling up his handiwork before placing it in his tunic pocket, Guido couldn't wait to show Michael what he had done.

Several days went by before they again found themselves together and minimally supervised in the garden, but when that occasion finally presented itself, the results were dramatic. After hearing Guido explain the concept of lines and spaces, in less than an hour Michael could repeatedly and consistently sing everything on the page. It was almost miraculous.

"It's amazing," said Michael. "You must share this with Brother Anselmo. Think how much easier his job will be!"

Guido agreed, resolving to bring the notated chant to Anselmo's rehearsal the next morning. Naively, and fully confident in the value of his idea, he had no inkling whatsoever of the torrent of troubles he was about to unleash.

Chapter Eight

CONTROVERSY IN THE CHOIR

The next morning, Guido could barely contain his excitement. He hadn't the slightest doubt that he had devised a practical solution to a very real problem, and he couldn't wait to share his discovery. After the office of Prime ended, he and Michael exchanged a look of eager anticipation.

As Brother Anselmo was collecting his chant book and monochord in the chapter house for the morning's rehearsal, Guido tagged alongside him.

"Brother Anselmo, I humbly beg your permission to show something to the choir this morning," he said. "It's an idea I had that I think would aid you in teaching us music."

Wrinkling his brow, Anselmo could not imagine how his procedures could possibly be improved, but he assented readily enough. After all, he now considered Guido his likely successor. "Of course, Brother Guido. I'm intrigued to hear what you have to say." With that he summoned the monks' attention.

"Brothers, one of your own, Brother Guido, has my

permission to address you. I have no idea what he wishes to offer, but please give him your respectful attention."

"Thank you, Brother Anselmo," said Guido with a slight bow before turning to the full assemblage. "Brothers, we have all experienced difficulty in learning new chant melodies."

Not you, thought Michael.

"The task involves memorizing a long series of musical pitches. There is no alternative to learning the note sequence by ear. And the only way to do that is by rote imitation. Any neumes above the words in the chant book are a useful reminder once the melody has already been learned, but their positions on the page are too vague to be of any use in learning the melody for the first time."

Judging by the mutters of approval, a good many of the monks seemed to be in sympathy with Guido's ideas so far. But Anselmo interjected with mild impatience, "Yes, yes, we all know this. You are merely describing what we do and have always done."

Smiling broadly as he prepared to unveil his innovation, Guido went on. "Each chant consists of only seven pitches—A, B, C, D, E, F, and G, with a possible eighth pitch repeating the lowest pitch up an octave. When the notes are lined up in ascending order, they form a stepwise scale. I have devised a method of notating those exact pitches for any chant melody so that you can learn a new chant simply by following the notes on the page, just as you learn words by reading the letters on the page."

This drew an audible murmur, prompting Anselmo to pluck

his monochord repeatedly to recapture the group's attention. Meanwhile Guido pulled out the scrap of parchment where he had notated *Ubi caritas* and held it up so that as many of the monks as possible could see it.

"I will pass this from hand to hand so you can each examine it more closely, but even from a distance you can see that the music is written on a grid—a staff—consisting of four horizontal lines. Neumes may be written either on the lines themselves or in the spaces between the lines. Each line or space represents a note of the scale, and each ascent to the next higher line or space represents the next upward step. Colored lines and initial letters indicate which of the four lines represent the notes C and F. So once you know your starting pitch, everything is spelled out precisely."

Anselmo listened to this oration with mounting irritation. "If you are quite finished, we will resume our rehearsal as planned," he said evenly, feeling his authority severely threatened. "Brother Guido, please take your seat and put away that piece of parchment."

"But—" began Guido.

"Did you not understand my instructions?" asked Anselmo pointedly.

Crestfallen, Guido silently took his accustomed place among the choir. Anselmo announced a new chant from the chant book, struck his monochord, and began the rote-learning exercise exactly as usual. And also as usual, in almost every phrase, at least one monk—most often Michael—would echo Anselmo's rendition inaccurately and fall prostrate in contrition.

But as the drudgery dragged on, the monk standing just to the right of the thus-far-unheralded inventor of musical notation gave a silent signal that he would like to see the parchment sheet Guido had intended to circulate. Once he had it in hand, this monk examined the notation with great interest, nodded enthusiastically to Guido, and then quietly handed the sheet to the monk to his right. At the risk of being disciplined, monks continued to surreptitiously pass the parchment around the choir. Anselmo, his head buried in his chant book as usual, remained oblivious.

The rehearsal ended only when the bells rang for the office of Prime. But during the brief interval between Prime and morning Mass, the disappointed Guido was approached by a younger monk, Brother Simoneto, who had concealed the parchment sheet inside a sleeve of his robe. Muscular in build, with a thick tonsure of jet-black hair, Simoneto gave Guido a conspiratorial smile. Disguising the handoff as a fraternal greeting, he transferred the sheet back to its creator.

"I think this is a wonderful idea," he whispered. "And so do a lot of the other brothers, especially the younger ones. It would make learning new chants so much easier."

"Thank you, Brother Simoneto," responded Guido. "If there really is that much enthusiasm among the brotherhood, I will try to bring up the idea again tomorrow. Perhaps it just takes Anselmo a little longer to consider new ideas."

But at the start of the next morning's rehearsal, when Guido respectfully mentioned that many of his fellow monks were interested in pursuing his notational ideas, Anselmo became even testier.

"And many of the monks would like to eat meat every day," he snapped. "That does not mean that it is right to do so. Please take your place so that I can proceed with my liturgical duties."

Guido shook his head in frustration as he fell into line. From across the choir, Michael gave him a look of dejection.

"I'd rather not bring this up at the chapter meeting," said Anselmo, pacing heatedly in a private conference with Prior Pangratio. "After all, I consider Guido my probable successor. No one else in all my years at Pomposa has ever matched his musical talents. But what he is proposing would render every chant book in the entire abbey obsolete. Inscribing new notation for all of the chants we sing would rob many hours from our daily labors, which are already stretched to the limit. And what becomes of my position as cantor and master of the choristers if the brothers could learn the melodies from a book? I feel like King David felt when his son Absalom rebelled against him! In my opinion, the whole thing is the work of the devil."

The imposing prior nodded grimly, offering no rebuttal. "Let us wait and see. Perhaps this will blow over on its own. After all, you have made it plain that what Guido has proposed will not be tolerated."

"Thank you, Lord Prior," said Anselmo, but he left the conversation feeling no less agitated.

As for Pangratio, on later reflection he recalled that another of the abbey's monks was Guido's uncle. He subsequently found an opportunity to warn Cristofano that Guido needed to abandon his absurd notational ideas immediately. Cristofano submissively promised to relay the warning to his nephew.

The next midday meal proceeded as usual. The monks sat eating in silence while Dom Guido as abbot read from the Rule of St. Benedict. But when the meal ended, as the monks were dispersing to their various work assignments, Cristofano steered his nephew into the cloister.

"Guido, you must give up your ideas about notating music," he said softly but firmly. "Brother Anselmo has been teaching the chants to the monks for many years. You learned from him yourself. He is teaching us the way monks have taught singing for generations, and the old ways have always worked perfectly well."

"But the old ways *don't* work well," retorted Guido. "Monks can spend weeks, months, even years failing to confess their errors before they finally learn exactly how to sing a new chant."

"Why is that your concern? You almost never make an error in singing."

"I'm trying to help my fellow monks."

"That is Brother Anselmo's concern. And he has made it plain that he does not wish for you to interfere."

"But the old ways don't work and my way does! Why should I keep quiet when I know I'm right?"

"Guido, I am greatly distressed to hear you speak like this. Please meditate on your errors and correct your behavior."

Deliberately ending the conversation, Cristofano turned and disappeared down the covered walkway.

Guido shook his head sadly and made his way to the kitchen, where he was assigned to shell peas. He tried to focus on the sheer manual labor at hand, but his thoughts kept returning to the highs and lows of the last few days. Taking out his frustrations on a pea pod, he tore it open with such violence that all the peas fell out onto the floor.

Observing silence as usual, his fellow monks said nothing but pointed to the runaway peas as Guido crawled on hands and knees to pick them up.

The abbey is certainly making good use of my talents, he thought ruefully.

Another morning, another music rehearsal, and another new chant to be learned: *Veni, Creator Spiritus.* As usual, Guido had little trouble absorbing the long sequence of notes from beginning to end, but also as usual, other monks floundered, especially Michael. Guido could not help imagining how much easier the task would be if this melody, too, were notated on his four-line staff.

Later that day, leaving the refectory after the evening meal, Michael begged Guido not to give up on his new ideas. "Please write out today's new chant," he pleaded. "And try one more time to change Brother Anselmo's mind. Otherwise I might as well spend all of every rehearsal on the floor."

Between Michael's entreaties and Guido's own innate sense that his ideas were worthwhile, the decision to persist was all too easy. Early the next morning, between Matins and Lauds, Guido sat in a dimly lit corner of the dormitory and wrote out every note of *Veni, Creator Spiritus* as Anselmo had introduced it the previous day.

This time, looking ahead to the morning rehearsal, Guido came up with a new strategy, which he communicated to a few sympathetic monks with whispered asides before and after Lauds. Those monks passed the word to others, so by the time the rehearsal began in the chapter house, nerves were distinctly on edge.

"Good morning," said Anselmo, greeting the choir with forced cheer. "Do we all remember *Veni, Creator Spiritus?*"

Some monks tentatively nodded, others fearfully shook their heads.

"Well, we'll soon find out, won't we?" continued Anselmo. And with that he struck the opening pitch on the monochord.

"*Veni, Creator Spiritus,*" he sang.

"*Veni, Creator Spiritus,*" all but a few monks sang back.

"*Mentes tuorum visita,*" Anselmo continued.

"*Mentes tuorum visita,*" came the response, but not as strongly as before—because those who weren't sure of the pitches were now merely mouthing the words.

"*Imple superna gratia,*" sang Anselmo.

"*Imple superna gratia,*" sang even fewer of the monks, as more and more of them dropped out.

Anselmo frowned but went on: "*Quae tu creasti, pectora.*"

Only a few scattered voices echoed, "*Quae tu creasti, pectora,*" but Anselmo pushed ahead all the more stubbornly.

"*Qui diceris Paraclitus*," sang Anselmo, almost shouting.

"*Qui diceris Paraclitus*," sang only a solo voice: Guido's.

Anselmo stopped abruptly. "What is the meaning of this?" he exclaimed in exasperation.

"Since you have asked us a question, I will endeavor to answer it," Guido piped up in his most conciliatory tone of voice. "As always, the old way of teaching a new chant melody is a slow and laborious process. Can't we at least try an alternate approach? Since yesterday I've notated *Veni, Creator Spiritus* completely, and if the others would like to look at what I've written—"

But Brother Anselmo was marching toward the door, his loud footsteps echoing on the tiled floor. All stood in uneasy silence as they watched him disappear.

"Since Brother Anselmo has left us to our own devices, please gather around," said Guido finally, trying to disguise his inward glee at the success of his experiment. "I've used a larger piece of parchment so that more of you can see the notation at the same time."

Brother Simoneto and other monks surrounded him enthusiastically, but several of the older ones—notably including Cristofano—stood to one side and glowered.

"Let's begin by singing the seven notes of the scale that make up this melody. Sing it after me," he instructed, and using the appropriate letter names, he intoned the seven-note sequence. After the monks repeated it, he had them sing only the first two pitches of the scale sequence, stopping on the second note.

"That second scale degree is the pitch of the chant's first

syllable, '*Ve-*.' It's represented here," he pointed, "on the lowest space of the staff. Now as I point to each of the neumes I've written on the staff, follow along and sing the first phrase slowly, one note at a time."

At a funereal pace, tentatively but with increasing confidence, they followed the written notes and sang with Guido: "*Ve-ni Cre-e-a-tor-or Spi-ri-tus.*"

"Yes!" exclaimed Guido excitedly. "Now the next phrase."

But before they could continue, Brother Anselmo reentered and loudly announced, "This rehearsal is over. Brother Guido, we will discuss this matter at today's chapter meeting."

For a moment, everyone stood in awkward silence. Then, avoiding eye contact with each other, the monks dispersed at random, knowing that within less than half an hour, they would all need to reassemble in the church to sing Prime and morning Mass. Only Cristofano held back for a private word with Anselmo.

"I am sorry for my nephew's intransigence," said Cristofano. "At the prior's request, I did my best to dissuade him."

"Please repeat that information at the chapter meeting," said Anselmo tersely.

Guido had learned that monastic life was a matter of routine. And the beginning of that morning's chapter meeting was indeed as usual, with the abbot leading an opening prayer and then reading a chapter from the Rule of St. Benedict. But for Guido, the remainder of the meeting was anything but routine.

When the abbot asked if any monk had an issue to bring

before the brotherhood, Anselmo immediately stood. "Lord Abbot, I have a complaint to bring against young Guido."

Clearly this was the first the abbot had heard of any trouble involving the monk who shared his name. Frowning slightly, he asked, "What is your complaint?"

"Lord Abbot, as cantor it is my designated responsibility to prepare the monks to sing in our Divine Office and Masses," began Anselmo, clearly agitated. "I learned my methods from the late Brother Domenico, who in turn was taught by his predecessor, and so on back to the founding of this community of faith."

The abbot nodded and Anselmo continued. "As an aid in singing the hymns, songs, and canticles, each monk is given a copy of our chant book, painstakingly copied out in our scriptorium."

The abbot let out a heavy sigh, not yet having heard anything he did not already know. Anselmo cleared his throat before going on.

"But Brother Guido has the temerity to believe he can improve on the time-honored methods that have served us so well for generations. He openly challenges my authority, claiming he knows how to do my job better than I do. What he proposes would mean discarding every single one of our chant books and replacing them with books that would be vastly more time-consuming to copy. He has sown unrest among the monks, encouraging them to resist my leadership. I simply cannot continue my work if this rebellion is allowed to continue."

The abbot's frown was now deeply creasing his forehead.

"Before we hear from the alleged offender, are there others who wish to comment on this matter?"

Cristofano stood. "I would like to add that Guido has continued to challenge Brother Anselmo as recently as today, despite receiving a warning from Prior Pangratio, as transmitted through me."

The abbot turned for confirmation to the prior, seated on his right, who silently nodded.

For a moment the room was quiet. Michael looked around, hoping someone would come to Guido's defense, and then hesitantly stood when no one else did.

"I wish to say that I have found Guido's ideas helpful in learning new chants," he said softly. "And I believe that others of the brotherhood have found them helpful as well."

But even Brother Simoneto and the other monks who had encouraged Guido privately, and who had crowded around him earlier to learn *Veni, Creator Spiritus* from his notated version, now saw which way the wind was blowing and remained guiltily silent.

"Brother Guido," the abbot asked, "what do you have to say in your defense?"

Challenged for the first time by his spiritual father, Guido stood momentarily speechless, reluctant to show disrespect. But his faith in his own ideas quickly won out.

"I have this," responded Guido calmly, holding up his parchment copies of *Ubi caritas* and *Veni, Creator Spiritus*. "With your permission, I will demonstrate the effectiveness of my methods."

The abbot beckoned him forward and Guido strode to the

front of the room, also carrying his copy of the traditional chant book, which he opened to *Veni, Creator Spiritus.*

"Lord Abbot, compare the melody as written in the chant book with the melody as I have notated it exactly on this sheet of parchment. The old way provides only the words and vague hints about how high or low each pitch should be. My way shows exactly which note of the scale should be sung for each syllable. Perhaps you would like to try it for yourself."

But there he made a strategic error, for the abbot was inherently insecure about his own musical abilities and was not about to let himself be put on the spot.

Gazing up imploringly at Anselmo, the abbot asked, "Is there anything to any of this? I . . . I am not qualified to judge in such matters."

"Lord Abbot," responded Anselmo gravely, "what Guido has done is completely unnecessary. It is merely a monument to his own sense of cleverness."

The abbot inhaled deeply. "Brother Guido, here we celebrate the sacraments the same way the Holy Church has celebrated them for hundreds of years. And no differently, we sing the divine liturgy as the Church has done for centuries. As the leader of this community, I am loath to challenge the teachings of our illustrious forebears. The old ways are always best. You will beg forgiveness for your errors, and henceforth you will respect the authority of Brother Anselmo."

"I do not believe it is an error to try to help my fellow monks learn music," said Guido combatively, eliciting a gasp from the assemblage. "But I submit to your judgment as our spiritual father and beg your pardon for interfering with the work of Brother Anselmo." With that he fell to his knees and prostrated himself before the abbot.

Utterly disheartened as he lay with his forehead pressed to the floor, Guido thought sadly, *Was this the future my mother imagined for me?*

Chapter Nine

AN OFFICIAL VISIT

Brother Anselmo's rehearsals resumed as before, with Michael repeatedly asking forgiveness for errors and Guido stifling his urge to intervene. Guido's heart sank every time Michael dropped to the chapter house floor in penitence. The sorrow he felt on his friend's behalf was even more painful than the disappointment he felt at the abbot's rebuke.

It was not until a cool, cloudy afternoon several days later that the two friends next found themselves laboring together outdoors. When their work eventually brought them both into the tool shed, Michael addressed his friend in a low voice.

"Guido, please," begged Michael. "Would you be willing to give me the parchment sheets where you wrote out *Ubi caritas* and *Veni, Creator Spiritus*? That way I can at least be sure I know those two chants perfectly."

"Of course," answered Guido with a sigh. "After all, I notated them to help you."

"Thank you! But unfortunately, I need a whole lot more help than that—help that I'm never going to get."

"I definitely saw what a difference the notation made for you," said Guido, clearly deep in thought. "I wonder—"

"Are you thinking what I'm thinking?" asked Michael.

In fact, he was. "What if I notate more chants, just for you? As long as you're always on your guard when you study the pages, so that no one can see what you're looking at, what harm would be done?"

"Guido, that would be such a blessing!" said Michael. "I promise I'll be very careful."

"Anytime I get a chance to write out a new chant, I'll leave it under your pallet in the dormitory," said Guido. Then, cautiously poking his head out of the shed entrance, he added, "Now wait here a few minutes so no one sees us leave together."

During his sessions in the scriptorium, Guido was obliged to focus on his assigned task—ironically, making a new copy of the old, imperfect chant book. But early every morning in the dimly lit dormitory, between Matins and Lauds, he would sit as far in the shadows as possible and work on notating new chants for Michael. Because it was a time for private labor and reflection, none of the other monks paid any attention to the nature of his activities. With his excellent ear and firm theoretical grasp, Guido was able to write out a new chant almost every day.

The trickiest part was finding an opportunity to leave the parchment sheets for his protégé. At least Michael's straw pallet was positioned along a wall rather than out in the middle of the long, open dormitory room. Initially, Guido tried being the last monk down the back stairs for Matins, but often the monk assigned to make sure everyone had woken up was still poking around. Guido enjoyed better luck returning to the dormitory ahead of all the others, since approaching footsteps would warn him when his window of opportunity was about to end. And at other times he carried a newly written parchment sheet beneath his rope belt so he could take advantage of any auspicious chance that might arise on the spur of the moment. But that was dangerous too, since the sheet sometimes slipped out and drifted to the ground at awkward times, forcing Guido to inexplicably kneel so as to conceal the music beneath the folds of his cassock. He always said a quick prayer while he was at it, both to disguise his intent and to give thanks for not being detected.

One way or the other, eventually the notated chants ended up beneath a corner of Michael's pallet. He typically retrieved the parchment sheets for study between Matins and Lauds —the same early morning period when Guido was writing out new ones. For Michael to be using this private time to work on learning chants scarcely surprised any of his fellow monks, given his persistent rehearsal difficulties. As long as he was completely surreptitious when taking out and returning the sheets to the growing pile beneath his pallet, all was well.

Brother Anselmo could not help but notice that Michael's errors were gradually becoming less frequent, but he attributed this improvement to his own tried-and-true methods.

"You see, Brother Michael," he remarked in a cheery aside as one morning's rehearsal ended, "I knew you would start to catch on eventually."

Michael merely smiled and hurried on his way.

~

It was while this clandestine musical activity was afoot that a messenger arrived at the abbey with a letter from Bishop Cunibert of Forlì. This official missive announced that Pope Benedict VIII had entrusted Cunibert with the responsibility of visiting the religious institutions across the Papal States—the jagged band of territories, at least nominally under papal control, that extended diagonally across the Italian peninsula, stretching north from Rome through Umbria and into Romagna. Cunibert's letter gave the date of his impending arrival—a mere three days away—and decreed that his dozen-man entourage of clergy, scribes, and servants would need to be fed and quartered for the duration of his stay.

Visiting inspections were a new development in the Roman Church, and this official visit was a first for Pomposa. Caught off guard by the news, Dom Guido summoned Prior Pangratio and shared the bishop's letter.

"What should we do?" asked the abbot, much perturbed.

"Do we have a choice?" responded the prior.

"Might we consider declining to receive the delegation?" wondered Dom Guido, sounding out his associate. "For some . . . pressing reason."

"We could say our resources are tied up with harvesting the crops," suggested the prior.

"But most of the wheat harvest is already complete."

"What about grapes? We could say we're busy making wine."

The abbot briefly considered the idea but finally shook his

head. "I see no alternative. God is sending us this visitation, and we must accept God's will."

Prior Pangratio bowed respectfully and awaited further instructions.

All aflutter, the abbot gave orders to ready the guesthouse for the arriving dignitaries and to warn the kitchen of the additional mouths to be fed. As a sign of special welcome, prompted by the prior's proposed excuse, he sent for several jugs of the abbey's best wine.

At the next morning's chapter meeting, the abbot described the visitation as a special honor bestowed upon Pomposa and urged all the monks to be as cooperative as possible. Unsure about the extent or potential consequences of the inspections, the monks all gave way to mounting uneasiness.

"Michael, can you hide the music parchments under your blanket?" asked Guido tensely. "Anything concealed on the floor might be discovered."

"Of course," answered Michael.

So that night, enveloped by darkness after all torches and candles had been extinguished, he carefully made the transfer. Brother Tomaso, whose pallet was just a few feet away, was still awake and could not help overhearing this furtive activity.

The big day arrived, and the entire population of the monastery was on hand to greet Bishop Cunibert—a pot-bellied, beetle-browed prelate whose horse was clearly straining under his weight. After dismounting and signaling for his entourage to do the same, Cunibert bowed and kissed the ground at the abbey entrance, then rose to greet Dom Guido, who kissed the bishop's hand. The abbot escorted Cunibert to occupy his own chamber, electing to humble himself by sleeping in the dormitory for the duration of the visit. Once the rest of the retinue had been shown their quarters in the guesthouse, everyone assembled in the chapter house, where Cunibert preached a long introductory sermon about the monks' sacred responsibility to God and the monastic community.

Concluding his prepared remarks, Cunibert then proceeded to his standard questions.

"Is the Rule of St. Benedict being observed?"

"Yes, my lord, we follow the Rule faithfully," responded Dom Guido.

"Do you all agree?" the bishop asked the assembly. Offering a sly smile, he added, "While I am here, you are always free not to agree with your abbot."

But the monks murmured their assent, so Cunibert posed his next question.

"Are the rites of the Divine Office being sung regularly and properly?"

"Yes, my lord, eight times a day we faithfully offer the liturgy of the hours," said the abbot with confidence.

Again, the monks indicated their agreement.

"Has the abbey experienced any recent disturbances or infractions?"

Guido grew tense, worrying that his attempts at notating chants might be mentioned. But apparently a more recent affair was considered more pertinent: A brother had been discovered hoarding salted meat and eating it on the sly in the kitchen.

"A recent violation of our dietary restrictions," said Dom Guido reassuringly, "but the matter has been attended to and the perpetrator sentenced to a lengthy fast."

"Otherwise," asked Cunibert, "do you feed and clothe yourselves from the common resources?"

All audibly assented, and the bishop seemed satisfied for the present. "Please retire to the dormitory and make sure the premises are clean and in order," he said before consulting briefly with the abbot.

Guido, Michael, and the other monks hurried to their quarters and toiled vigorously until the entire chamber was spotless from one end to the other. Just as they were putting away their brooms and mops, the bishop and abbot appeared and proceeded to inspect the room from top to bottom. The monks stood uncomfortably along the walls, each fearful of being accused of some unimagined infraction.

"Who has failed to straighten and smooth his blanket?" asked Cunibert, grabbing a tangled woolen coverlet.

"It was I," an older monk apologized. "I was busy sweeping the floor and ran out of time."

"Don't let it happen in the future," muttered the bishop, handing off the blanket as he continued through the room.

The chastised monk hurriedly smoothed out his pallet and resumed his place along the wall.

"What is this? An article of personal property?" asked Cunibert sternly on discovering Guido's earthenware chalice.

Before Guido could even begin to respond, the abbot intervened. "He has my permission to retain this one personal article," said Dom Guido. "It was blessed at his investiture. He presented it as an offering, but I allowed him to keep it."

"Very well," said Cunibert, moving on. Rummaging under the rough blanket that covered Brother Tomaso's pallet, his hand sensed something round. He held up a ripe pear. "Whose is this?"

"This is where Brother Tomaso sleeps," said the abbot apologetically.

"Brother Tomaso," said the bishop, "you are ordered to fast until my departure from the abbey."

"Yes, my lord," said Tomaso, dropping to his knees. But then he noticed Cunibert was about to walk right past Michael's pallet.

"Aren't you going to check that one as well?" asked Tomaso innocently. "I heard some strange sounds from there the other night."

"All right, let's take a look," said Cunibert, kneeling to feel his way up and down the pallet. Toward the foot, he sensed something interrupting the expanse of coarse straw. Reaching under the blanket, he triumphantly pulled out the pile of parchment manuscripts.

"What is this?" he asked, genuinely puzzled. "There should be no need to conceal materials for personal study."

But the abbot, looking over his shoulder, immediately suspected the nature of the discovery. "Brother Anselmo, could you come here, please? Take a look at these pages."

As a low murmur of apprehension spread across the room, Anselmo marched over to join the bishop and abbot.

"Brother Anselmo, is this not the forbidden work of Brother Guido?" queried the abbot.

"It is, my lord," said Anselmo, needing only a cursory glance to confirm his suspicions.

"Lord Bishop," said the abbot angrily, "Brother Guido has caused great dissension in the abbey by refusing to accept the musical authority of Brother Anselmo and by claiming to write out music in a new way that would overthrow centuries of sacred tradition. He had confessed his fault before the full assembly, and I thought the trouble had been put to rest. But apparently he has been continuing this sinful work behind my back, and Brother Michael has been his accomplice."

"Lord Bishop," said Michael timidly, "these pages have been a great help to me in learning to sing the Divine Office without error. I beg you to consider the value of what Brother Guido has done before you condemn us."

"But you have clearly disobeyed your superiors," responded Cunibert brusquely. Handing the stash of parchment to the abbot, he said, "Keep these manuscripts as evidence. I will address the matter later."

Guido and Michael shared a forlorn look. Then both bowed their heads, all too conscious of the disapproving stares of their fellow monks.

For the remainder of the day and much of the next, Cunibert

continued his inspection, scrutinizing every aspect of the abbey's operations and every corner of its complex of buildings. He consulted privately with the abbot, the prior, the librarian, and other monks in positions of responsibility. In one respect, the visitation was a pleasant break in the monastic routine: Meals were a special treat, with the finest foods and wine placed on the tables in commemoration of the bishop's presence. But even while enjoying these generous repasts, all the monks felt anxious about the progress of Cunibert's examinations. And none were more anxious than Guido and Michael.

At last the hour arrived for the bishop to again summon the full assembly in the chapter house, this time to hear his final report. Cunibert began by complimenting the abbey and its leadership on—in general—conscientious adherence to St. Benedict's Rule and the Divine Office. He spelled out various procedural corrections that needed to be implemented, droning on about minor details of the vestry and library until half the monks were lulled to the brink of sleep. But they suddenly jerked to attention when he abruptly changed his tone.

"The one thing that has most deeply disturbed me is the discovery that one of your membership, Brother Guido, has been violating the strict orders of your abbot and flouting the authority of your choir master by inscribing forbidden copies of the liturgical chants in a highly irregular fashion," stated the bishop firmly. "I have learned that this monk's musical rebellion has created much discord among the brotherhood, and that his supposed contrition was apparently a sham. Another monk, Brother Michael, has actively encouraged Brother Guido in his sinful endeavors and has brazenly attempted to conceal the evidence of their misdeeds."

As Cunibert paused to take a deep breath, a voice was heard from the back of the chapter house.

"Lord Bishop," said Guido, daring to step forward, "if you could take a moment to look at what I have done, I believe you would realize that my method greatly improves on the old ways of learning music, and that—"

"Silence!" shouted Cunibert. "Brother Guido and Brother Michael: Kneel before me."

The two slowly made their way to the front of the room and fell prostrate to the floor at the bishop's feet.

"Brother Guido, you have violated your vow of obedience and have led a younger brother into sin. You are indefinitely barred from notating music or teaching your heretical method to others. You are both to withdraw separately from all inter-action with the community for forty days, during which time you are banned from participating in the public liturgy—with the exception of the sacraments, which will remain accessible for the benefit of your souls. When you rejoin the community, you are never again allowed to work in the same area of the abbey at the same time."

Someone must have seen us talking in the garden and tattled on us, thought Guido wearily.

Guido and Michael dropped their heads even lower, their dejection complete. Then they slowly dared to turn toward each other and exchange a look of mutual despair, each trying to express without words that he felt worse for the other.

"This concludes my report," said Cunibert, and he and the abbot marched officiously from the room.

The hulking Prior Pangratio pulled Guido and Michael to their feet, grabbed them both by the wrist, and silently escorted them to their separate places of confinement in a distant area of the abbey.

As he entered his tiny cell and heard the door lock behind him, Guido thought, *Perhaps Uberto was right to run away.*

Chapter Ten

AN UNFORESEEN OPPORTUNITY

Guido stoically endured his forty days and nights of isolation. His waking hours were spent praying, meditating, and reading the copies of the Bible and St. Benedict's Rule that had been placed in his lonely cell. He availed himself of the opportunity to confess his sins within the sacrament of penance, to attend a private daily Mass, and to receive the Holy Eucharist. His only brief moments of human contact came when a servant unlocked his door—no monk was permitted to attend to him—to bring his daily allotment of bread and water or empty the chamber pot. Because no sunlight penetrated his cell, Guido used these visitations as a rough guide to the time so that he could still solitarily celebrate the canonical hours eight times a day.

When Guido prayed, his entreaties were twofold. First, he asked God for wisdom—to help him understand why his notational procedures were sinful. Deep inside, Guido still regarded his ideas as valuable and constructive, even ingenious. And no matter how often he prayed for understanding, throughout the full forty days of his incarceration he was unable to shake that conviction.

Even more fervently, Guido prayed for forgiveness—for having led Michael into sin and punishment along with him. And even though he eventually began to feel forgiveness from above, he still found it most difficult to forgive himself. *If I hadn't kept giving music to Michael,* he thought, *at least he wouldn't be getting punished like I am.* It was this consciousness of his friend's suffering that tortured him more than anything else.

At last, after Guido had begun to lose track of the passing days, his cell was unlocked and the usual servant escorted him through the cloister, where he could see that dawn had not yet broken. Despite the early hour, he was led directly to face Dom Guido.

"Brother Guido, have you profited from your days of penance?" asked the sleepy-eyed abbot, wearily following his usual post-punishment routine.

"I have, Lord Abbot," replied Guido, kneeling at his feet. "I ask your forgiveness."

In saying so, he was sincere—but only as it applied to leading Michael astray. Despite all his prayers to the contrary, Guido still could not help but believe that his musical ideas required no forgiveness whatsoever.

"By the authority of our Lord Jesus Christ, and through the mercy of the Blessed Virgin Mary, I absolve you of your sins in the name of the Father, and of the Son, and of the Holy Spirit," intoned the abbot. "Amen."

Guido rose, bowed deeply, and was led to the dormitory,

where Michael had been escorted shortly beforehand. In the central chamber, the other monks were engaged in their usual private study and meditation before Lauds, and they all scrupulously avoided meeting Guido's gaze. He and Michael exchanged a momentary glance in bleak silence.

After the midday meal, as the monks were filing out of the refectory, Michael tentatively approached his mentor.

"Guido, can you ever forgive me?" whispered Michael, beckoning him toward the cloister. "If I hadn't asked for your help, you would never have been disciplined and punished. The whole time I was in confinement, what tormented me the most was knowing that I had caused you to suffer the same punishment."

"Michael, what most tormented me was that you were suffering for my misdeeds," answered Guido intensely. "I'm the one who wrote out the music. Of course I forgive you, but can you forgive me?"

"There's nothing to forgive," said Michael somberly. "As long as I live, I'll be grateful for everything you did for me, and for all the risks you took for me."

"I regret none of it," said Guido. "I only wish I could have helped you more."

Fearful of inviting new accusations, they exchanged a quick look of mutual sympathy and went their separate ways. But in trying to end their friendship, the abbey had instead cemented their lifelong bond.

For Bishop Cunibert, Pomposa had marked the northernmost extent of his visitational jurisdiction. From there, he and his retinue headed south to Comacchio, where he inspected the Monastery of Santa Maria in Auregiario. After stopping to pay a courtesy call on his superior—Eriberto, archbishop of Ravenna—he proceeded south to visit the Abbey of Santa Maria del Monte in Cesena. Heading west for one additional inspection before reaching his home cathedral in Forlì, Cunibert examined Badia Abbey in Bertinoro. The issues he confronted on these stops were relatively routine: Monks eating meat too frequently, sleeping on feather mattresses instead of straw mats, keeping forbidden personal possessions.

His return to Forlì was brief, for in continued fulfillment of Pope Benedict's mandate, he was soon resuming his tour of inspection. Heading south, Cunibert visited the Camaldoli Monastery in Poppi, where discipline was so lax that most monks were being allowed to sleep through Matins. From there he moved on to the Abbey of San Michele Arcangelo in Verghereto, where he was obliged to mediate a property dispute with an adjoining manor, and then to the Monastery of St. Bartolomeo, within the ancient walled center of Anghiari. In a serious breach of the Rule of St. Benedict, several monks there had fathered children in clear violation of their vows of chastity.

Before proceeding even further south to visit the Hermitage of San Cataldo in Rieti, he paid another courtesy call—this one to a fellow bishop, Theodaldus, at the Cathedral of St. Maria and St. Stefano in Arezzo. Relaxing at an opulent luncheon offered in his honor, Cunibert regaled his host by sharing tales from his various visitations.

"I saw little toddlers in the school at St. Bartolomeo, and

some of them were girls, so I knew they couldn't all be oblates," said Cunibert, shaking his head. "Sure enough, they turned out to be the bastard children of some of the monks."

Theodaldus—tall, bald, and solidly built—gave a weary sigh.

"I made certain that the offenders renewed their vows of chastity and performed appropriate penance," said Cunibert, "though I suspect a return visit may be in order."

"The spirit is willing, but the flesh is weak," observed Theodaldus.

"This was scarcely the first such case I've encountered, and I fear it won't be the last," continued Cunibert. "But I did see one thing on this expedition that I'd never come across before. In Pomposa, one of the monks had come up with an entirely new way of notating chant melodies. He claimed it would help the monks learn music more easily, but the whole affair had thrown the abbey into complete turmoil."

Cunibert paused for another succulent bite of roast fowl before resuming his anecdote. "The cantor supervising the singers was upset, and the prior didn't want to have to replace all the old chant books, so I had no choice but to stop the whole idea dead in its tracks." With that he lifted his goblet to his lips for a generous gulp of wine.

But Theodaldus's interest was piqued. The singing master at his cathedral had recently died after years of failing health, so the choir's musical training had declined to the most rudimentary levels. Truth be told, by now the singing of the boys and men—which years earlier had so inspired young Guido—was downright embarrassing. Theodaldus realized that the Cathedral of St. Maria and St. Stefano could make good use of someone who could teach music to the singers more effectively and efficiently.

"This monk at Pomposa devised a new way of teaching singers to learn the chants?" he asked, clearly intrigued.

"So he said. He even tried to get me to examine his chant notation. And one of the other monks claimed that this new system had been a great help to him."

After another sip, Cunibert went on, "But what could I do? If you ever heard me sing, you'd know I'm scarcely competent to render judgment in such matters. And both of them had flagrantly disobeyed their superiors."

"What was the name of the monk who came up with this new way of notating music?" asked Theodaldus with feigned nonchalance.

"His name?" said Cunibert, straining to remember. "It was . . . oh, yes, it was Guido. The same as the name of the abbot there."

The next morning, after Cunibert and his entourage had departed for the monastery in Rieti, Bishop Theodaldus summoned a servant from the rectory.

"Oliverio, I need you to bear a message to the abbey in Pomposa," said Theodaldus eagerly. "I will provide you with two horses and ample provisions for the journey, as well as letters of introduction to monasteries along the way where you will be housed and fed. When can you be ready to begin the journey?"

"May I wait to leave until dawn tomorrow?" asked the

designated emissary, realizing that the trek would be long and arduous.

"As you wish," said the bishop. "But I will have the letters written for you within the hour."

As weeks and then months passed at Pomposa, Guido was increasingly miserable. Music rehearsals with Brother Anselmo were now pure agony, both because Guido constantly had to witness Michael abasing himself and because he knew without a shadow of a doubt that his own approach was greatly superior. He kept his head down, singing the hymns and psalms accurately but without spirit. The thought that this situation would continue unchanged for the rest of his life filled him with gloom. Adding to his anguish was the ongoing disapproval of the abbot—the man he considered his spiritual father—and the impossibility of ever exchanging more than a few passing words with Michael. He prayed for wisdom, for serenity, and for strength, but his prayers seemed to go unanswered.

Then early one spring afternoon, he was summoned to see the abbot. The sudden command filled Guido with deep apprehension. Although he had completely refrained from attempting to write out any more chant melodies, he worried that perhaps some fellow monk, still resentful of his musical rebellion, had concocted a tale claiming that he had. Or maybe other monks had noticed that he was merely going through the motions of his devotional duties. Was the abbot about to discipline him for his poor attitude? His thoughts swirling mercilessly, Guido uneasily made his way into the abbot's chamber.

"*Benedicite*, Lord Abbot, you asked to see me?" asked Guido, bowing respectfully. Looking up, he noticed a roughly dressed layman standing off to one side.

"I have received a letter from Bishop Theodaldus at the Cathedral of St. Maria and St. Stefano in Arezzo," said the abbot, choosing his words carefully.

Guido had not thought of the Arezzo cathedral for many years. But with this unexpected mention, his mind was flooded with the wonderful memory of listening to the choir's angelic voices at the special Mass celebrating the new millennium.

Clutching the bishop's letter in one hand, the abbot now drew it up to his field of vision and reviewed its contents before resuming his remarks.

"The bishop has invited you to assume a position training the cathedral's singers. He is . . . ."—the abbot uncomfortably cleared his throat—"he is interested in having you use the musical notation that you developed here as an aid in teaching the liturgical chants. It seems he heard about it from Bishop Cunibert, who recently visited Arezzo."

Although the abbot's stern gaze scarcely betrayed his true feelings, he in fact had been delighted to receive this surprising news. Brother Guido had ended up being nothing but trouble, the cause of serious friction at the abbey. Out of the blue, here was a diplomatic way to eject him.

"Therefore," said the abbot with appropriate finality, "I direct you to leave the abbey and take up your new post in Arezzo."

Guido stood dumbfounded. Sequestered from the outside

world since he was a mere child, he was now nearly thirty. Though he had become increasingly unhappy at Pomposa, it was the only adult life he knew. Now, in effect, he was being banished from the community that had become his home. He was frightened of the unknown and apprehensive about life outside the protective walls of the monastery.

And yet, despite his severe punishment at Pomposa, Guido had never lost faith in the value of his ideas. Here, finally, was an opportunity to make use of his notational methods, in an environment where they would be not only tolerated, but welcomed. And he would be training the very choir whose singing so inspired him as a boy.

"Thank you, Lord Abbot," answered Guido at last. "I am grateful for the invitation." After silently thanking God for this unexpected answer to his prayers, he could not help thinking of Michael. "Might I be allowed to bring my fellow offender with me?" he asked. "As my assistant?"

Dom Guido had already foreseen this question and had prepared his answer. In the abbot's view, Guido and Michael had stirred up enough trouble together at Pomposa; the Holy Church would be better off if the two were separated. Speaking calmly but decisively, the abbot replied, "I will require that Brother Michael remain at Pomposa."

Guido's heart sank. Finally, he asked, "How—and when— am I to take up my post?"

Indicating the unfamiliar layman who had stood quietly throughout this interchange, the abbot said, "This is Oliverio, the bishop's servant. He has brought two horses so he can escort you to Arezzo. He would like to leave immediately in hopes of reaching Comacchio before dusk."

Wordlessly, the emissary stepped forward and offered Guido a small leather satchel for the journey.

The suddenness of the imminent departure dealt Guido a whole new shock, and for a moment he stood paralyzed, trying to think of everything he would need to do in his last few minutes at the abbey.

"I will gather my possessions," he said at last, taking the satchel and turning to leave.

"Wait," said Dom Guido, opening a drawer in a rough-hewn chest. "Take these with you." As if expelling a vile contagion, he handed Guido the forbidden stack of parchment sheets where he had notated music for Michael.

"Thank you," said Guido, unexpectedly moved to regain his handiwork. Stuffing the pages into the satchel, he added, "May God bless you and all the brotherhood."

"And may God bless your journey," said the abbot, relieved to end the awkward encounter.

After arranging to meet Oliverio a few minutes later at the bell tower, Guido nodded his final farewell to the abbot. Not only would he now never regain his spiritual father's approval, but in all likelihood, he would never even see him again.

Guido hurried back to the deserted dormitory, where he found the crate containing his few possessions. He quickly packed his quill, inkhorn, knife, and writing tablet, unsure how readily available those items would be at the cathedral. And in a dusty corner of the crate, he spied his father's "Guido" chalice. Finding a rag near the mops and brooms, he used it to carefully wrap the cup and then placed it in the satchel.

Though loath to keep Oliverio waiting, Guido knew that he might never return to Pomposa. Surely he could not leave forever without saying goodbye to the friend with whom he had endured so much persecution. But where might Michael be at this hour?

Guido methodically crisscrossed the complex—the cloister, the kitchen, the refectory, the chapter house, the library, and the sacristy, even the lavatorium. At least he knew he could skip the scriptorium, since both he and Michael had been banned from working there. Other monks were going about their labors throughout the abbey, and since none of them knew he was leaving, Guido refrained from saying goodbye; any explanation would be left to the abbot. But no matter where he searched, there was no sign of Michael.

Increasingly agitated, Guido ran out to the garden, the scene of so many fateful meetings between the two friends. Scanning the area, he finally spotted Michael picking berries near one of the outbuildings. Guido raced toward him, completely out of breath.

"Guido!" exclaimed Michael, thoroughly yet pleasantly surprised to see him. "But won't this get us into more trouble?"

"It doesn't matter now," panted Guido. "In a few minutes I'm leaving here forever. I've been invited to train the singers at the Arezzo cathedral. The ideas that I developed to help you can finally be brought out into the open."

Michael stared blankly as he gradually took in the startling news. At last he blurted out, "What a blessing for you. You'll be so much more contented there. I know how miserable you've been here."

"I wish I could bring you along."

"To help train singers?" exclaimed Michael, grinning despite his distress. "That'd be a joke."

"I pray that we will meet again," said Guido softly.

"Surely we will," said Michael, with more hope than conviction.

For a moment they stood facing each other in silence, each growing sadder as he sensed the depth of the other's grief.

"I must go," stammered Guido. "My escort is waiting at the bell tower."

Again they stood motionless. Then, impulsively, they did something they had never done in all their years of friendship: They threw their arms around each other in a tight fraternal embrace. Finally letting go, the two monks reluctantly drew apart.

"Goodbye!" called Guido as he set off in a trot toward the bell tower.

"Godspeed!" shouted Michael, his eyes misting as he watched his dearest friend recede in the distance and finally disappear from view.

Chapter Eleven

A NEW START

As Guido hurried toward the bell tower, he could see the bishop's servant pacing impatiently alongside the two saddled horses. A monk was waiting there as well, and as Guido came closer, he recognized Cristofano, his tonsure now flecked with gray. The two had not spoken to each other since Cristofano had sternly warned his nephew to abandon his musical innovations.

"The abbot told me you were leaving," called Cristofano as Guido drew near. "I wish you Godspeed on your journey. I hope you will be happy in Arezzo."

"Thank you," said Guido, struggling to catch his breath.

"I'm sorry that your life at Pomposa did not turn out as well as you would have liked," added his uncle solemnly.

"I have learned to serve God and the Church," replied Guido. "That should prepare me for whatever lies ahead."

His escort mounted one of the horses and gestured for Guido to take the other.

"If you're ever able to return to Talla, please convey my best wishes to our family," said Cristofano as Guido climbed into the saddle.

"I will. Goodbye!" shouted Guido, grateful for this moment of reconciliation, as the horses began moving down the pathway.

It had been two decades since Guido's parents had made the long journey to bring him from Talla to Pomposa. Now he was returning to the territory of his homeland, an area he had never expected to see again. He actually viewed the lengthy trek to Arezzo as a blessing; at least the days en route would ease the suddenness of this unforeseen transition.

The bishop's servant focused on navigating the route to Comacchio, so initially the two riders proceeded in silence. Accustomed to spending most of his time without speaking, Guido at first was content not to talk. But then he had a sudden, surprising realization: The day's abrupt change of course meant that he could now talk freely whenever he pleased. For someone as outspoken as Guido, this came as a happy discovery.

So as the distance from Pomposa gradually increased, Guido attempted to make conversation. "Your name is Oliverio?" he asked.

"Yes, Brother Guido."

Hoping that his guide might be a helpful source of information about his new place of occupation, Guido asked, "Tell me, what sort of man is Bishop Theodaldus?"

"I would say the bishop is kind and generous," answered Oliverio slowly. "And unlike many of the clergy, he seems open to new ways of thinking."

He must be, if he's inviting me to train his singers, thought Guido.

"But sometimes he's too caught up in his own ideas to notice what's happening right under his nose," the servant continued.

"What sort of things?" asked Guido, genuinely curious.

"I don't know if I should tell you," said Oliverio, turning away to face the path.

"This is the first time I've been outside a monastery in twenty years," confided Guido. "I need to learn as much as I can about my new situation if I'm to make a success of it."

"Well, some of the priests are guilty of simony," ventured his companion.

The term was unfamiliar to Guido. "Simony?"

"They sell things that shouldn't be sold—ecclesiastical positions, pardons from sin, even things they claim are sacred relics."

"But do they give the money to the Church?"

"No, it goes into their own pockets. And Theodaldus either doesn't know what's happening or else chooses to look the other way. He doesn't like confronting people."

So this is what it will be like to live in the outside world, thought Guido ruefully, suddenly realizing how different his existence would be from a monastic life of service and contemplation.

"What do you do at the cathedral?" asked Guido, trying to shift the conversation to a less awkward subject.

"My wife and I are servants in the rectory. We do the everyday work, taking care of the household."

"And do you have any children?"

"A little boy, two years old."

"A boy!" exclaimed Guido. "Perhaps when he's older, he'll sing in my choir."

"Oh, no, Brother Guido. He's just a peasant boy, unworthy to sing in the big cathedral."

"If he can sing, bring him to me," said Guido. "Do you promise?"

"As you wish," said Oliverio, giving his horse a slap.

The two travelers reached Comacchio by late afternoon and quickly located the rough stone walls of the Monastery of Santa Maria in Auregiario. Thanks to Bishop Theodaldus's letters of introduction to abbeys along Oliverio's route, the messenger had enjoyed the hospitality of Santa Maria's monks the previous night. Now the brothers there warmly welcomed Oliverio's return and were delighted to receive a fellow monk as his traveling companion.

The Santa Maria monks stabled the two horses, provided the two visitors with a generous repast (no doubt more lavish than the meal they had just eaten themselves), and then led them to the guest quarters—complete with feather mattresses. Guido had ridden horses and donkeys as a child and occasionally when working in the more distant fields at Pomposa, but the afternoon's ride had left him quite sore, so he was content to revel in this unaccustomed luxury.

The next day Oliverio and Guido journeyed from dawn to nearly dusk, with the monk now peppering his guide with questions about Arezzo. How many boys were in the choir? (Currently only half a dozen.) How many priests served at the cathedral? (As few as six or as many as eight, with minor clergy coming and going.) As master of the choristers, where would he live? (The priest who previously held the post had been provided with his own room in the rectory.) Did Bishop Theodaldus manage every detail of the cathedral's affairs, or did he give his subordinates free reign? (Oliverio didn't feel qualified to answer the question.)

At last they reached the next monastery where Theodaldus had arranged for their accommodations, the Abbey of San Mercuriale. Located outside the walls of Forlì, this abbey too had received Oliverio on his trip north. Again treated to abundant hospitality, the visitors enjoyed another refreshing night's rest.

"We should be able to reach Arezzo before sunset," said Oliverio as the two set off the next morning.

Guido, as usual, let his guide lead the way—until he began to notice a few vaguely familiar sights as the day wore on. At a recognizable fork in the road, he suddenly reined in his horse, prompting Oliverio to stop as well.

"Oliverio, I think the road to the right is the way to Talla."

"I believe that is correct. So?"

"Talla is where I was born," explained Guido. "As far as I know, my family still lives there, but I haven't seen them in twenty years. Do you think Bishop Theodaldus would be upset if we stopped there for the night and arrived in Arezzo a day later?"

"The bishop's instructions make allowances for unforeseen delays."

"Would *you* mind?" asked Guido.

"My wife and son had hoped to see me tonight. But I am at your service."

"I'm sorry, I don't want to delay you," said Guido. "We can go on."

"No, Brother Guido," said Oliverio good-naturedly. "I've seen my family much more recently than you've seen yours."

With Guido following his lead, Oliverio steered his horse toward the righthand fork.

At Pomposa, as a monk vowing to forsake the outside world, Guido had largely banished any memories of his childhood. But as he approached his hometown, they all came flooding back: the fields and the forests, the smell of wet clay, the heat of the kiln, the aromas of his mother's cooking, the teasing of his brothers, and most of all, the spinning of the potter's wheel.

Entering Talla with Oliverio, Guido pointed out the little parish church, still looking much the same as before. But several of the dwellings and other buildings he remembered had long since vanished. It was with increasing apprehension that he led the way toward his old home.

The cottage was still there, with the ramshackle pottery shed still intact, and even a new lean-to on the opposite side. Dismounting a discreet distance away and tethering their horses to a tree, the two travelers walked warily toward the cottage, with Guido leading the way.

As he drew closer, Guido heard the reassuring hum of the potter's wheel. The shed was open, so he stepped hesitantly toward the entrance and peeked in. Two men were at work, one shaping clay on the wheel and the other glazing pottery. It took Guido a few moments to realize that they were his brothers.

"Bertoldo? Bernardo?" called Guido.

Bernardo paused in his glazing and took a step toward him, while Bertoldo looked over his shoulder as he continued to mold the clay. Who could this unknown monk be who had mysteriously appeared at their door? At first they stared at him without any sign of recognition, but then Bertoldo noticed something familiar in the visitor's bony, angular face. Suddenly he exclaimed, "Guido?"

"Yes!" said their long-absent brother, stepping forward to embrace Bernardo.

Bertoldo quickly brought his latest clay creation to a premature finish and then turned to hug his brother as well.

"This is Oliverio," said Guido, gesturing toward his guide, who was still standing outside the shed. "He's bringing me to the cathedral at Arezzo, where I'll be training the choir."

"You must both stay with us tonight," said Bernardo. "It'll be crowded, but we'll make room."

"Where is Father? And Mother?" asked Guido.

His brothers looked at each other solemnly. Finally Bertoldo said, "Soon after you left, Mother was with child again, but this time she didn't make it . . . or the baby either."

"Oh, no!" exclaimed Guido.

"Then last autumn," Bertoldo continued, "Father got the fever. We thought he was getting better, but right before Christmas, he passed on."

"I'm so sorry," said Guido. "I wish I had known."

"Both times, we wanted to let you know," said Bernardo, "but we weren't sure how to get word to you."

After a moment of heartfelt silence, Guido asked, "And how are the two of you?"

"I married Ysabel, Father's cousin's daughter, and we have a little boy," said Bertoldo. "Bernardo got a girl from the village in the family way—"

"Stop!" said the grinning Bernardo, seeing no reason to air dirty linen.

"Anyway, they're married now too, and have a little girl. So there are six of us here—that's why we built the new lean-to."

"Uncle Cristofano is still at the monastery at Pomposa," said Guido, recalling his last conversation by the bell tower. "He said to give you his best wishes."

"Thanks," said Bernardo. "I have a vague memory of meeting him."

"Remember when we tried to cut off the hair on the top of your head?" asked Bertoldo with a jab to Guido's ribs. "And now you keep it cut off yourself."

As Guido smiled at the memory, Bernardo said, "Come along and meet your new relatives." Seeing Oliverio still waiting at a distance, he added, "You, too!"

"I'm sorry," said Guido to his guide as they entered the cottage. "You're going to have to listen to a lot of catching up about people you don't know."

Guido talked more in that one evening than he had spoken in twenty years at Pomposa. Over a plain but ample meal, he recounted all his joys and travails at the monastery and listened as his brothers and their wives shared news of the last two decades in Talla. Finally the two couples and their children crowded into the tiny bedroom and let their visitors sleep in the even tinier addition.

The next morning, strangely exhilarated by this unexpected reunion, Guido bade farewell to his family and went on his way with Oliverio, knowing he might never see any of them again.

Reaching Arezzo by horseback was an easy half day's journey. As they drew closer, a whole new set of childhood memories resurfaced for Guido—the trip to the cathedral for the Mass celebrating the new millennium, and the angelic sounds of the choir as it sang for the service. He still found it hard to believe that he would now be part of that tradition.

At last, outside the city walls, they neared Pionta Hill. Since Guido's boyhood, the once-dilapidated Cathedral of St. Maria and St. Stefano had been extensively renovated. So as the imposing Romanesque structure came into view, Guido gasped in surprise at its refurbished exterior. After the horses were tethered, Oliverio started to escort the monk directly to the rectory to meet the bishop, but Guido asked if he could visit the cathedral first. Receiving his guide's assent, and carrying the satchel containing his few possessions, he walked alone across the portico and opened the tall, heavy doors.

Before him, lit by dozens of candles and by the sunlight streaming through a row of high windows, lay the central nave, with its lofty vaulted ceiling and its twin borders of rounded archways. Guido said a silent prayer of gratitude, then knelt and made the sign of the cross before rising to rejoin Oliverio outside.

Leading Guido to the rectory, Oliverio said, "This completes my mission. I wish you joy in your new labors."

"Thank you, and thank you for escorting me here safely," responded Guido. "And remember what I said about your son."

Oliverio nodded and smiled, then knocked on the rectory door. An older male servant answered and immediately said, "You must be Brother Guido."

Moments later, the newcomer was ushered in to meet Bishop Theodaldus. The tall, bald cleric, appearing to be about the same age as Guido, stepped forward and offered his hand in greeting, smiling broadly.

"Brother Guido, I'm delighted to welcome you," said the booming voice.

"Lord Bishop, thank you for this call to serve you," said Guido, kneeling.

"Please, no need for that," urged the bishop jovially as he helped the monk to his feet. "I'm the one who should thank you. Your skills and knowledge are much needed here."

"I look forward to putting them to good use," answered Guido, already feeling comfortable in the bishop's presence.

"You arrive here at an exciting time," said Theodaldus. "About twenty years ago, the celebrated architect Adabertus Maginardo helped renovate our cathedral. I've recently commissioned him to create a whole new chapel here to be dedicated to

St. Donatus, who, as you may know, was martyred in Arezzo. Here, let me show you the plans."

Reaching into a tall pine cabinet, the bishop pulled out several large sheets of parchment and spread them on a table. Guido gazed admiringly at the drawings, noticing the semi-circular apse, the rounded arms of the transept, and the small hexagonal skylight in the center of the sloping roof. As in St. Maria and St. Stefano, the nave was to be bordered on each side by a row of rounded arches, here supported by slender double columns.

"Most impressive," said Guido appreciatively. "And not only that, but I see your parchment is of the highest quality. May I make a request?"

"Of course," answered the prelate. "What do you need?"

"As an essential supply for my work, I will require as much blank parchment as you can spare. And I'll need more sheets every day."

Not batting an eye, the bishop replied, "I'll have some delivered to your quarters this very afternoon. Speaking of your quarters, let me show you around."

With that, Theodaldus led the new arrival to a high-ceilinged room in the rectory, furnished with a feather mattress, a simple cupboard, a table, and a bench. Guido marveled at both the unaccustomed privacy and the room's size, bigger than his family's entire cottage in Talla.

"Why not go ahead and leave your things here?" suggested the bishop.

Guido emptied his satchel, taking special care to place the sheaf of parchment pages on the table. Then, even more carefully, he unwrapped the "Guido" chalice and set it in a safe place on a shelf in the cupboard.

Continuing to the school, adjacent to the cathedral, Theodaldus showed Guido the music room, where he would be training the singers. A monochord rested on a table, and scattered chant books lay on the wooden benches.

"Brother Guido, this is entirely your domain," said the bishop. "You have free reign here to teach however you choose."

Though life at the cathedral was to bring its own share of trials, at that moment Guido truly felt that he had died and gone to heaven.

Chapter Twelve

CATHEDRAL VOICES

Since the demise of the cathedral's previous singing master, a haphazard succession of priests and minor canons had tried to fill in, and the most recent of these was all too glad to be relieved of the responsibilities. So, on that first evening, knowing that he was expected to begin his duties the very next morning, Guido kept his candle burning into the late hours as he notated new sheets of chant melodies. The cathedral's music sessions were scheduled during the intervals between the rites of the Divine Office; he would be teaching the boy choristers in the mornings and rehearsing the men's choir in the afternoons.

Before the morning session, Bishop Theodaldus met Guido and escorted him to the music room. Watching his half-dozen young charges filing in, Guido felt a surge of nervous excitement about finally putting his methods into actual practice.

"Young gentlemen," the bishop announced forcefully, "this is Brother Guido, a Benedictine monk. He is your new singing master. In this room, what he says is gospel."

The boys looked variously intrigued, bored, or mildly defiant.

"Brother Guido, I leave you to your work," said Theodaldus, making a brisk exit.

After fixing his gaze on each boy in turn, Guido broke the silence. "Good morning," he said, and the choristers—trained in rote repetition—all replied, "Good morning."

"Do you have your chant books with you?" asked Guido mischievously.

The boys nodded and held up their bound collections.

"Excellent," said Guido. "Hand them to me. You won't be needing them."

Suddenly puzzled, they nevertheless did as they were told. Guido was tempted to start a bonfire and burn the old books to ashes, but he resisted the dramatic gesture and merely placed the volumes in a neat pile by the window.

"Now gather around the table and look at this page," he said, setting out a large parchment sheet for their inspection. It bore a single four-line staff with a neume on each line and space, starting on the lowest line and continuing up by step across the page. Guido pointed out that the second line from the bottom was red, indicating the note F, and the top line was yellow, indicating C. Beneath the staff were the letter names corresponding to each of the notes: D, E, F, G, A, B, C, D.

"Every hymn, every canticle, every psalm, every responsory we sing is built from these few notes," he said. Then, after sounding a D on the monochord, he sang the pitches one by one while pointing to the corresponding note on the staff.

"Sing them after me," he said, and the boys did so, following Guido's finger as he pointed to each new note in turn.

"Now here are the same notes, but arranged in a different order," said Guido, flipping to his next parchment sheet. This time, as he pointed out, the second-to-bottom line was yellow (C), so the notes ran from A through G and on up to the higher octave of A. Guido plucked an A on the monochord and led the boys in singing this form of the scale.

"The staff can be arranged in different ways, depending on which lines are C and F," Guido instructed. "But once you know that starting point, every note that you sing can be notated exactly by its position on a line or space."

The boys stared intently at the staff, their brains working feverishly.

"So if we go from one note to a higher note," asked a precocious lad, "the lines and spaces will show us exactly how many steps higher to go?"

"And we don't just have to guess?" chimed in another, remembering the discarded chant books' vague changes in neume heights.

"Precisely," said Guido, further energized by these responses. "Now let's look at an actual chant melody that some of you may already know." On his next sheet he had notated *Benedicamus Domino*—the first melody he had learned by rote from Brother Anselmo, and the chant that with its response, *Deo gratias*, concluded each of the eight liturgical hours.

"Here again," said Guido, "the second line from the bottom is yellow. And the first note is on that yellow line. So that note is—?"

"C?" said one of the boys tentatively.

"Correct!" exclaimed Guido, who proceeded to sound a C on the monochord. "Now sing the notes slowly, one by one, as I point to the neumes on the staff."

And so they did. The next time through, they added the words. When they came to the end, the boys all looked at each other and burst into laughter.

"It's so much easier this way," said one boy happily.

"Where did you learn all this?" asked another.

Guido paused. Humility had always been his greatest challenge. Finally he said, "By the grace of God, and through the gift of His blessings . . . I devised it myself."

The boys' eyes grew wide. They were so impressed with their new teacher that from then on, discipline in Guido's classroom was rarely a problem. Before the first day was out, the young choristers could sing a whole new hymn by following Guido's precise notation.

With the young men singers, Guido began with a different approach. He started by introducing a complex, little-known hymn melody in the old way—by singing it and asking the singers to repeat it. As he expected, they all stumbled at some point in the very first phrase. Resentful that their new teacher seemed to have begun by deliberately humiliating them, they all grudgingly began to fall to the floor to confess their errors.

"Stop! Stand up!" said Guido, smiling. "Wouldn't it be better if there was an easier way to learn music?"

The choir members looked at each other, now thoroughly confused.

"And in fact, there is," he continued, directing their attention to his parchment sheets showing the scales starting on D and A. Guiding them through the principles of his system just as he'd presented it earlier to the boys, Guido soon had the adult choir learning the new hymn with surprising confidence. At the end of the rehearsal, several singers stopped to thank him.

"It is I who should thank you," he replied. "You have given me confirmation that I'm on the right track."

That night Guido was so exhilarated that he could barely sleep. Reliving all the events of the day, he thought, *If only Brother Michael could have been here to see this.*

When Guido arrived in Arezzo, Palm Sunday was only a few weeks away, but in just a few rehearsals he had taught the boys their music, especially *Gloria, laus*—the hymn they were to sing in procession while waving palm branches. The special service required unfamiliar chants for the men's choir as well, but by the time the day arrived, all were fully prepared. It was the first major showcase for Guido's work since beginning his new position, and both choirs performed impressively. Although Bishop Theodaldus had engaged Guido with high expectations, even he was amazed by the rapid improvement in the cathedral's music. Easter was an even greater triumph.

Guido drew immense satisfaction from at last being able to prove—on a daily basis—the effectiveness of his methods. And leading the choirs in Mass and the Divine Office, he was constantly gratified to be offering music to others in the same holy space where he had first come to love music himself. Invigorated by notating more and more music for daily Masses and the Divine Office, he occasionally composed new chants of his own. He also experimented with organum—splitting a choir so that half the singers improvised at a consistent interval (a perfect fifth or fourth) above or below the original melody.

At times, amid the hustle and bustle of the cathedral, he missed the private meditation and quiet contemplation of monastic life. And whenever he saw a priest smugly rattling coins after meeting with a parishioner, Guido was disgusted by the unethical goings-on. Most of all, he missed communing with Brother Michael, his friend and kindred spirit. Yet whenever he recalled the stifling conformity of Pomposa, he uttered a prayer of thanks that he had been able to escape. And every time his blunt pronouncements in the music room were met with the usual respectful acquiescence, he knew he was in the right place. As a sign of satisfaction with his new situation, after remaining clean-shaven for his entire adult life thus far, Guido permitted himself to grow a beard—at least partially concealing the sharp angles of his bony face.

Bishop Theodaldus was true to his word and let Guido pursue his work without interference. So the monk was understandably curious when, after a year or so at the cathedral, he was unexpectedly summoned to the bishop's chamber. As he entered, Guido saw that Theodaldus was holding a well-worn book.

"I'm sure you know Boethius's *De institutione musica*," said the bishop without any preliminary small talk.

"Yes," said Guido, "I studied it when I was a boy in school at the monastery."

"This was written five centuries ago!" exclaimed Theodaldus.

"There have been more recent theoretical treatises," said Guido. "*Musica enchiriadis*, for instance."

"But I feel sure that your understanding of musical principles extends beyond any existing book."

"I cannot disagree," responded Guido, never one to hide his accomplishments under a basket. "Many advances have been made."

"And many of them have been made right here in Arezzo, through your new methods," said the bishop excitedly. "I think the world needs a new book on the principles of music. And I think you're just the man to write it."

Although the suggestion was a complete surprise, it took Guido only a moment to embrace the idea. "I'm flattered by your proposal, and I'd be honored to share my ideas in writing," he said. Then, struck by the project's practical demands, he added, "But won't this require a great deal of my time?"

"I've thought of that already. I'm commissioning you to write this book, so it's now a priority of your work here. You can train one of the more experienced men in the choir to serve as your assistant so you don't have to teach as much. And I'll assign one of the canons to be your scribe so you can dictate, if you'd prefer."

"Thank you, Lord Bishop," said Guido happily. "And so now I'll be needing even more of those blank sheets of parchment."

Laboring over the following months, Guido produced twenty chapters for a book he named *Micrologus* (*Little discourse*). He dedicated it to his patron, Bishop Theodaldus, praising him specifically for the marvelous plan of the Church of St. Donatus, which by then was under construction.

Conscious of his book as a successor to both *De institutione musica* and *Musica enchiriadis*, Guido nevertheless declared that his work was not a philosophical, purely theoretical treatise. Instead, it was intended as the first-ever guide to the actual practice of learning chant—a summary of "certain things I believed would be helpful to singers." He wrote, "Let whoever seeks our training study these rules, so that after learning the notes' effect and character, he can with ease sing both familiar and unfamiliar music." His dedication to Theodaldus described the book's methods as so effective that, in the practice of music, "even boys at your cathedral should surpass fully trained veterans everywhere else."

Beginning with the idea of *vox* (voice) as sound, he assigned the letters A through G to the different musical tones, referring to the notated sounds as *nota*. Starting on a low G (gamma), he laid out a twenty-pitch gamut of ascending steps. ("One could continue the pattern up or down indefinitely," he added, "but the precept of art authoritatively restrains this.") Next, Guido classified the usable intervals between notes—the semitone, whole step, minor third, major third, perfect fourth, and perfect fifth—and specified the ratio for dividing the monochord to produce each interval. He noted the "affinity" between certain notes—how, for example, the sequence of scale tones from D to A (ascending by the interval of a perfect fifth) corresponded exactly to the equivalent five-note sequence from A to E. Tying these observations into the overall seven-note hierarchy, he added that "affinity is only perfect at the octave," where all patterns in a higher octave exactly repeat those of the lower.

Guido went on to explore the possibilities of melodic motion created by moving upward or downward at each possible interval. And he identified the final note of a chant as a likely indicator of its primary pitch. He then explored the various patterns that resulted when each of the different pitches functioned as that tonal center.

Guido continued by relating the structure of chant to the structure of speech, defining chant as sung speech. Further asserting that a chant's character should reflect the meaning of its text, he offered pioneering guidance in how to improvise and compose new melodies.

In discussing organum—the practice of adding a parallel part above or below the melody—Guido innovatively offered options for oblique and contrary motion between voices. This proved to be a particularly prophetic aspect of his treatise, pointing the way toward the independence of simultaneous voices in polyphonic music.

At last, after nearly a year of work, Guido presented the finished book to its dedicatee. Paging through the beautifully notated manuscript, Bishop Theodaldus was ecstatic.

"I predict that this book of yours will become the most important musical treatise of our day," exclaimed the bishop.

"And to make sure that happens, we must have additional copies made immediately. You are authorized to use as many scribes as you need to get it done."

"Thank you for providing the time I needed to complete the book," said Guido, much relieved by the bishop's reaction. "Now, of course, I can relieve my assistants of the burden of handling some of my teaching and rehearsing."

"Not so fast," said Theodaldus, raising his eyebrows. "You need to move on to your next book."

"My next book?" asked Guido, genuinely puzzled. "What would that be?"

"Don't worry, you've already done a great deal of it, with all the chants you've notated for our singers. Just keep writing out more psalms and hymns and canticles, and then put all of the pages together to make a new chant book."

"A new chant book!" said Guido excitedly. "And when I'm finished, can we make copies of that too, so every singer has his own copy of all the music we sing?"

"Not only that, we'll make copies to send to other cathedrals and monasteries," said Theodaldus enthusiastically. "A good idea deserves to be spread around."

And so Guido pulled together all the music he had notated at both Pomposa and Arezzo, wrote out more for use in future services, and organized the whole book so that singers could navigate it easily. Scribes quickly set to work making copies, first for the cathedral's choristers. But when Theodaldus reminded Guido that he wanted additional copies to send to other religious centers, the monk realized that his work as a writer was still not done. Encountering a volume as groundbreaking as this new chant book, outsiders would need a detailed preface explaining his methods. Returning to his parchment and quill, or pacing about while dictating to a scribe, he produced the *Prologus in antiphonarium* (*Prologue to a chant book*).

With characteristic bluntness, Guido began the *Prologus* by declaring, "In our times, above all men, singers are the most foolish." Bewailing the amount of time that choristers spent learning music by rote repetition, he asserted that without his method, "wretched singers and their pupils, even if they were to sing every day for a century, will never be able to sing one chant, even a short one, by themselves without a teacher." He lamented that learning one chant by rote made it no easier to learn another one. And because singers' training had always relied on trying to imitate the teacher, there was no uniformity even among the singers in a particular choir, much less between different choirs and different chant books. Only through exact notation of pitches, as in his new chant book, could any melody be sung in a definitive form. No longer feeling obliged to show false humility, Guido boasted that singers who mastered his system could learn music far more quickly than before, and even learn it on their own.

Offering specific details on how to use the book, he explained that the melodies were notated on a grid of lines, with each line representing pitches a third apart (two steps) so that the distance between a line and an adjacent space represented a step. "Thus the notes are so arranged that each pitch, however many times it may recur in a melody, is always found in the same row. To make it easy to distinguish these rows, the lines are drawn close to each other, so that some rows of pitches are placed on the lines themselves, and others in the spaces between the lines."

To identify which lines stood for which pitches, he gave the F and C lines the colors red and yellow, indicating the only two pitches whose immediate lower neighbors are a half step down rather than a whole step down. He also provided actual clefs—a letter at the beginning of a line to specify its pitch.

Guido tried reading the *Prologus* to his next new cohort of boy singers to prepare them for using his chant book, only to find that it was too complicated for the youngsters to easily understand. So, to provide the book with a more accessible introduction, he wrote a whole new treatise, presenting much the same information as the *Prologus* but this time in verse: the *Regule rithmice* (*Rhythmic rules*). He began it with an acrostic that was anything but self-effacing, spelling out his own name with the first letters of each line:

> *Gliscunt corda hominum mollita meis Camenis.*
> *Una mihi virtus numeratos contulit ictus.*
> *In celi summo dulcissima cantica fundo,*
> *Dans aule Christi cum munera voce ministri.*
> *Ordine qui dixi me primo carmina scripsi.*
>
> *(The hearts of men are gladdened, softened by my muses.*
> *My singular power has united the counted beats.*
> *In highest heaven I establish sweetest songs,*

Offering a gift to the courts of Christ with the voice of a servant. I who spelled out my name to begin each line am the one who wrote these verses.)

Using colorful imagery to communicate his principles, Guido compared a loud, piercing voice to a donkey that would drown out a nightingale, and suggested that there are seven basic pitches just as there are seven days in a week. When pointing out the necessity of clefs and colored lines for pitch orientation, Guido noted that without one or the other, the music "will be like a well that lacks a rope, making its ample water of no practical benefit."

For months and even years thereafter, scribes at Arezzo were kept busy making copies of all four of Guido's books. During this time, Bishop Theodaldus was much preoccupied with supervising the completion of the new Church of St. Donatus. But he greeted each of Guido's new volumes with unbridled enthusiasm, sending copies to nearby monasteries and making a point of showing them off to every distinguished visitor who passed through the city.

One such distinguished visitor was a papal legate returning from ecclesiastical business in Forlì. Theodaldus proudly introduced him to the cathedral's prized singing master, bragged about Guido's prowess in training choristers, and even gave the legate a copy of the chant book to take back to Rome.

Chapter Thirteen

A PAPAL SUMMONS

With the completion of the chant book and the three treatises summarizing all his innovations up to that point, Guido suffered an inevitable letdown. Without any urgent focus for his creative energies, and without the preoccupation of writing new books, he was increasingly drawn back into the day-to-day business of life at the cathedral. Overseeing the scribes' often careless copying of his writings soon became tedious, and the widespread graft among the clergy was continually dispiriting. He still enjoyed leading music for the services, and the angelic sounds of his well-trained choirs never failed to lift his spirits. But as one year gave way to the next, each bringing a new crop of untrained boys to be taught, he began to feel like Sisyphus, perpetually rolling the rock up the mountain and then starting again from the bottom.

One bright spot came at the start of a new liturgical year. As the fresh class of choirboys filed into the music room, Guido noticed Oliverio—the rectory servant who had brought him from Pomposa—standing in the corridor. With him was a tall, dark-haired boy.

"Brother Guido, remember you said to bring my son to sing in your choir?" asked Oliverio.

"Of course!" answered Guido.

"This is Luca," said the boy's father. "Sometimes after Mass, we hear him singing the hymns to himself."

Just like I did, thought Guido. Addressing the boy, he asked, "How old are you?"

"I'm seven," said Luca shyly.

"Perfect," said Guido. "Come in. Welcome to the boys' choir."

"Thank you!" said Oliverio, filled with emotion at the thought that his son would soon be raising his voice in the great cathedral.

Young Luca had a clear, sweet voice and an excellent musical ear. He progressed so rapidly that he was soon singing solos in services, inspiring his parents' pride and delight. Guido was already imagining that the boy could eventually become one of his assistants, perhaps even his successor.

And then one day, Luca and two of his friends dared each other to drink water from the fountain in the city's central plaza. They quickly developed dysentery, and one died within days. Another eventually recovered, and Luca too seemed to rally, cheered by daily visits from Guido. But one afternoon when the monk arrived at the infirmary, he was met by Oliverio and his wife, their faces stained with tears.

"No!" exclaimed Guido in panic.

"He is singing with the angels now," murmured Oliverio. "Thank you for all you did for him. He truly looked up to you."

Guido's eyes welled with tears. "I'm so sorry," he said, clasping Oliverio's hands. "Thank you for entrusting your son to me."

Luca's untimely death only deepened Guido's gloom, and he became more and more impatient and irascible. Incidents that he might have managed to ignore in earlier years now aroused his blunt outspokenness, which soon led to even more difficulties.

After Mass one morning, collecting the choir's chant books in the chancel, he noticed a peasant woman approaching the gray-haired Father Jacobo, one of the cathedral's longtime priests. Her clothes were little more than rags, but tied to her wrist was a small leather bag that appeared to be bulging with coins.

Continuing with his labors, Guido picked up a book that needed repair and then turned to leave. There was the peasant woman again, this time walking back toward the narthex. Her little leather bag was gone.

Turning quickly to the chancel, Guido spotted Father Jacobo nonchalantly rattling the bag of coins. The monk defiantly marched up to the priest.

"You should be ashamed of yourself," said Guido angrily.

"What does this have to do with you?" asked Jacobo, more surprised than upset.

"I am a servant of Christ and His Church."

"The lady's son had no future, and now he'll be a canon here at the cathedral," stammered Jacobo defensively. "I've done a good deed."

"And you've taken a poor woman's tiny savings to line your own pockets," retorted Guido. "The least you could do is give the money to the Church."

Jacobo snorted. "The Church didn't help her—I did."

"What servant of the Lord would enrich himself at the expense of the poor?"

"Most of the priests at this cathedral, that's who," laughed Jacobo. "I'm scarcely the only one."

Wearily, Guido realized that this was all too true. "You haven't heard the last of this," he warned before storming back to the rectory.

But when—without naming names—Guido brought the matter before Theodaldus, the usually forceful bishop became evasive.

"Perhaps you misunderstood," he cautioned. "Maybe the priest was going to use the money for alms."

"I think he would have told me if that were the case," argued Guido.

"I'll ask the provost to look into it," said Theodaldus vaguely. But on reflection he decided not to pursue the matter, preferring not to know what might actually be going on.

Father Jacobo, however, was not nearly so circumspect. He warned other priests about Guido's disapproval, with the result that they reduced their interchanges with him to the bare minimum necessary to conduct services. Though Guido retained the bishop's full support, he was essentially ostracized by most of the cathedral's clergy, who of course continued to commit simony and transact other unsavory business. For Guido, it was almost like being back in the oppressive atmosphere of his last days in Pomposa.

Those memories always made him think even more often of Brother Michael and the persecution they had endured together. Any time travelers visited the cathedral, Guido invariably asked if they might be going toward Pomposa Abbey. And for the few who answered in the affirmative, he always asked if they might relay his warmest greetings to Brother Michael, as well as to the abbot and Brother Cristofano. He had no way of knowing if the messages were ever delivered; he only knew that he had yet to receive any response. Worrying that Michael was still suffering from the stifling disapproval of his fellow monks, Guido felt his mood growing even darker.

So early one summer day when he was called before Bishop Theodaldus, Guido feared the worst. Perhaps the priests had conspired to have him dismissed from his post. Where would he go? What would he do?

Entering the bishop's chamber, he saw three strangers clad in red-accented robes that bore the papal insignia.

"Guido!" exclaimed Theodaldus cheerily. "I don't know if you were aware, but I sent a copy of your chant book to Rome. It was presented to His Holiness Pope John XIX, who was very much impressed. In fact . . . ." said the bishop, pausing to heighten the effect of his announcement, "he has summoned you to Rome to tell him more about your methods."

The monk was relieved to hear good news, but he recoiled at the mention of John XIX. From what he had heard about the Church in Rome, this pope was knee-deep in bribery and scandal. In fact, John was the brother of the previous pope, Benedict VIII, and their family was known for graft and simony. John had not even been a priest at the time he was elected to the papacy. He stood for everything that Guido adamantly opposed.

"I would be honored," said Guido finally, in spite of his misgivings. He was a servant of the Church, and the pope was the Church's earthly head, so he saw no other choice in the matter.

"I don't know how we'll manage without you," said Theodaldus candidly. "But I must bow to the pope's wishes. Let me know of anything you might need in preparation for your journey."

"Thank you," responded Guido. "As always I am deeply grateful for your support and encouragement."

The papal emissaries were treated to the bishop's warm hospitality, so they were content to stay two nights before departing for Rome. During that time, Guido worked closely to prepare Canon Francesco—his lanky, curly-haired senior assistant—to teach and rehearse the choristers during his absence.

Readying himself for the journey, Guido packed a new copy of his chant book, along with a copy of the *Prologus* and other notes. He stared for some minutes at the "Guido" chalice, still resting safely in the cupboard of his chamber. Should he bring it with him? What if it didn't survive the lengthy trek? Since he fully expected to return to the cathedral, he decided to leave it behind as a token of his plans to resume his duties.

Theodaldus had arranged for Guido to be accompanied by Dom Petro, the cathedral's learned prefect of the canons, and Abbot Grimaldus of the abbey at Badicroce, just south of Arezzo. Joining them and their three papal escorts, Guido set out on yet another long journey across the Italian peninsula. The boy who grew up never expecting to leave his native region was now extending the compass of his life to cover a diagonal swath from the northern Adriatic coast almost to the Tyrrhenian Sea.

Dom Petro was one member of the Arezzo clergy whose behavior had remained above reproach, and fortunately he had stayed on cordial terms with Guido. Along the way, the two enjoyed many lively philosophical and theological discussions, with Abbot Grimaldus chiming in from time to time as well. The three papal emissaries spent most of the journey gossiping about intrigue at the Holy See, but in tones too soft for the others to overhear.

The party's first destination was Perugia, where they soon spotted the distinctive hexagonal bell tower of San Pietro, a monastery founded only a few decades earlier. Arriving shortly before sunset, the visitors were settled in the guest quarters soon enough to allow Guido a quiet, meditative stroll through the cloister. *This is what I've missed*, he thought, sighing contemplatively.

The second day's journey brought the travelers to the Hermitage of San Cataldo in Rieti. Built in the face of a huge granite rock, the monastery sat nestled within the mountains, almost completely isolated from the outside world. Welcoming the visitors, San Cataldo's abbot silently showed them the abbey's Byzantine-style frescoes and its celebrated painting of the Redeemer flanked by apostles and saints.

After the evening meal, a few moments of conversation were allowed between the guests and their hosts. It was then that a younger monk approached Guido.

"Excuse me," he said. "I'm Brother Rizardo. Did I hear correctly that you are Brother Guido of Arezzo?"

"I am," answered Guido.

"I'm so honored to meet you!" exclaimed Rizardo. "We use your chant book here constantly, and our library has a copy of your *Micrologus*."

"Really!" responded Guido, genuinely surprised. He knew that Bishop Theodaldus had given out copies of his writings, but he little suspected how far and how quickly his ideas had spread.

"The notated music has made such a difference," continued Rizardo. "It used to take our monks such a long time to learn to sing all the chants correctly. Now, thanks to your methods, they learn everything so much more quickly."

"Thank you for the testimonial," said Guido warmly. "Working away at the cathedral, I've had no idea that anyone else was even using my system, much less that they found it valuable."

"I'm sure we're not the only ones. By now you're actually quite famous, you know," said Rizardo before respectfully withdrawing.

From this sole encounter, Guido was already gratified that he had undertaken the journey. Knowing that his methods were having a positive effect far afield from Arezzo gave him a renewed burst of confidence. And his spirits were refreshed by his moments of meditation back in a monastic environment.

When morning came, he was unexpectedly reluctant to leave the abbey. But now he genuinely looked forward to sharing his ideas in Rome.

As the party of six drew closer and closer to their destination, the summer weather grew warmer and steamier. By the time they reached the outskirts of Rome, the air was thick with noxious vapors arising from the surrounding swamplands. Guido, a child of the mountains, soon found himself coughing uncontrollably.

They continued to the Lateran Palace—the papal residence, located in the city's southeast sector at St. John's Square on the Caelian Hill, one of Rome's famous seven hills. The ornate structure sat adjacent to the historic Archbasilica of St. John Lateran, with its stone portico ornamented by two tiers of rounded arches. Dominating the square, larger than life, was a gilded bronze statue of a bearded Roman emperor mounted on his horse.

The papal emissaries conducted the three guests to the palace, where they were welcomed and escorted to richly appointed chambers. For Guido, who grew up in an abbey with a straw mat on a stone floor as his only bed, the contrast was startling. But beset with fever, muscle aches, and coughing, he was under the weather, more ill than he had ever felt in his life. Relieved to hear that it might be several days before he would be granted his promised audience with the pope, he took to his bed—the most comfortable one he had ever slept in.

Chapter Fourteen

A LESSON FOR THE POPE

The next day, as Guido lay ailing, he had ample time for reflection. From his stopover at San Cataldo, he knew that his once-condemned methods had by now begun to achieve considerable currency. If he recovered sufficiently to meet with the pope, and if His Holiness found merit in his ideas, they might spread even further. *This life is but a brief prelude to the next*, he thought. *If I must die here in Rome, I can die content that my work on earth is accomplished.*

But then his thoughts turned to Brother Michael; perhaps a response to Guido's messages might finally be on its way to Arezzo. He also remembered that he had left his father's chalice on the shelf of his cupboard in the rectory. Slowly, his resolve began to revive. *I must live so I can go back to the cathedral,* he told himself. *I must get well.*

Worried about Guido's health, Dom Petro asked to see him and was ushered into the monk's chamber.

"So now we know how the privileged live," said Petro in greeting, gesturing to the lavish quarters.

"Yes, and I suppose we shouldn't ask how it was all paid for," said Guido, rolling his eyes.

"How are you feeling today?"

"I'm slightly better," answered Guido. "Ordinarily I'd love to be outside, seeing more of this fabled city—the pines, the hills, the ancient ruins. But it's better for my health to stay inside, away from the fetid air."

"The vapors haven't affected me yet," said Petro, "but to be safe, I'm following your example and avoiding the outdoors as much as possible."

"How do you think I should I prepare for my papal audience?" asked Guido, moving directly to the subject on his mind.

"I'm sure you're prepared already," said Petro. "Just do what you do every time you start working with a new group of boys. You've explained your ideas to countless singers in person and in your writings, so you should have no trouble explaining them to the pontiff."

"But what do you know about Pope John?" asked Guido.

Petro paused before responding. "I'm sure we've both heard the same things. How he wasn't even ordained until after he was elected pope. How he reportedly bribed the cardinals to win the position. How his family is well known for unethical dealings."

Guido shook his head sadly. "To think this is who occupies the Chair of St. Peter."

"Of course, he can't be much worse than many of the priests at our cathedral," added Petro ruefully. "Maybe the Church got the pope it deserved."

"And God moves in mysterious ways," mused Guido.

"Maybe the Lord is preparing the way for reform by making it more obvious how much reform is needed. Even so, I'm not looking forward to meeting this fraudulent 'spiritual leader.'"

"But he must be a man of great discernment," said Petro with a wink, "since he's called you here to learn about your ideas."

Days went by, leaving Guido impatient to see the pontiff but also grateful for the additional time to recuperate. During the interim, he and his two companions were treated to lavish meals, typically including beef or poultry. At least the generous nourishment aided his recovery.

Finally, late in the afternoon of the fourth day after the visitors' arrival, an emissary appeared with the papal summons. Guido gathered his chant book, *Prologus*, and a few loose parchment sheets, then wrapped a scarf around his nose and mouth in hopes of protecting his lungs from the prevailing miasma.

Dom Petro and Abbot Grimaldus had been summoned as well, and the three were escorted out of the palace toward the basilica, walking past the equestrian statue on the way. Silently saluting the bronze horse and its rider, Guido thought whimsically, *I suppose both of you have to breathe this polluted air every day.*

The emissary led the trio not through the basilica's front portico but to a private entrance along the side that led toward the apse, its high concave ceiling decorated with brilliant mosaics of biblical scenes. Blazing candles illuminated the sanctuary from all sides. Safely indoors, Guido removed his scarf and gazed in all directions at the most magnificent cathedral he had ever seen.

Still many steps in the distance was the imposing papal cathedra, where a seated figure was surrounded by various canons and attendants.

"Welcome," shouted a rough voice from the direction of the pontifical throne. "Come closer so I can decide if I really want to talk to you." The greeting was followed immediately by a raucous laugh that echoed throughout the reverberant space.

Guido and his two associates looked at each other warily, then quickly approached the throne, occupied by a heavy-browed, bearded figure in full regalia. The glittering papal tiara rested on his head; the white linen alb, bright red mantle, and skirted *falda* extended past his ankles.

"*Benedicite*, Your Holiness," said Guido, kissing the ornate Ring of the Fisherman on Pope John's extended hand before kneeling at his feet.

"Get up, get up," exclaimed the pope. "I didn't bring you all the way from Arezzo just to look at the top of your head."

Still weak from his ordeal with the vapors, Guido set down his books and parchments but still faltered as he tried to stand. The pope himself took his hand and helped him up.

"Thank you, Your Holiness," said the monk breathlessly, retrieving his materials.

"And how was your journey from Arezzo? I trust my emissaries brought you here safely."

"Yes, Your Holiness. And our visits to the monasteries in Perugia and Rieti were most restorative."

"And your apartment in the Lateran Palace, is that satisfactory?"

"Oh, yes, Your Holiness," replied Guido, "though much too comfortable for a humble monk like me."

"Bah," said the pope. "You deserve the best of our hospitality. What about your meals? Are they to your liking?"

"I have never eaten so well in my life," answered Guido with complete honesty.

"I understand you've been ill."

Trying to play down his affliction, Guido answered, "I was born and raised in the mountains. I'm afraid this warm, damp air doesn't agree with me."

"I grew up breathing it, so I should be even sicker than you are," joked the pope.

"I hope not, Your Holiness," said Guido.

"So, you're in the service of Bishop Theodaldus at Arezzo, I believe? What do you think of him?" asked the pope before adding conspiratorially, "Don't worry, you can speak frankly with me."

"He is a great and good man," answered Guido. "Nothing I have achieved would have been possible without his unwavering support."

"I like to hear you speak well of your superior," said the pope, "whether he deserves it or not." He let out another raucous laugh; Guido forced himself to smile.

"So what did you bring to show me?" asked Pope John, indicating the books Guido was carrying. "I already have a copy of your chant book and it's really very fascinating," he continued, gesturing to an attendant to hand it to him.

"Not to boast, Your Holiness, but with my methods, a

singer can learn in five months what formerly would have taken ten years."

"Then that's exactly how I want our choirs here to be learning music. But I need you to show me how it all works."

"Could we bring in a few boys from the basilica choir?" asked Guido helpfully. "I could demonstrate with them the way I do with my own choir in Arezzo."

"No, no, no. No need for that. You can try it out on me."

"You want me to . . . to teach you to sing from this chant book?" asked Guido skeptically.

"That's right, that's right. Just like you'd teach one of your boy singers."

"I'll have to pick a hymn that you don't already know," said Guido, starting to page through the book.

"Oh, that should be easy. I hardly know any of them," said Pope John. "After all, I was never even a priest till I ended up here." Another raucous laugh.

Guido exchanged a quick glance with Dom Petro.

"But I have a good voice," added the pope, looking to his canons for confirmation. "I'm a good singer, aren't I?"

As they nodded obsequiously, the head of Christ's Church on earth began bellowing a bawdy ballad.

Quickly cutting him off, Guido interposed, "You're right, Your Holiness. You have a lovely singing voice."

The pope gave his canons a knowing nod.

As Guido flipped nervously through his chant book, he happened upon *Te Deum laudamus*. Considering it a good omen to begin with the first chant he had ever heard himself, Guido turned the book to face the pope.

"Have you heard this before? *Te Deum laudamus?*"

"No, never. I told you, it's all new to me."

"Excellent, Your Holiness. Now you'll see that above the words is a grid of four horizontal lines," explained Guido, finally getting down to the business at hand. "The grid forms lines and spaces, and each line or space stands for a specific musical pitch, represented by these neumes, the black dots either on the lines or in the spaces between the lines."

"Yes, I see what you're talking about," responded the pope, eyeing the page intently.

"There are four lines and three spaces, so they stand for a total of seven consecutive pitches, with the highest at the top and the lowest at the bottom," continued Guido patiently. "And the first two lines of this hymn are made up of five of those seven pitches."

"I think I'm following you so far," said John.

"Very good, Your Holiness. Now let's try singing these notes." Leafing through his parchment sheets, he found one notating the scale notes E-F-G-A-B-C-D-E. Not needing a monochord thanks to his excellent sense of pitch, Guido intoned the notes by their letter names from lowest to highest, pointing to the corresponding neumes on the staff as he sang.

"Now sing with me," Guido continued, and as he again pointed to the neumes in succession, the pope sang along with the monk, hitting all the scale notes perfectly.

"I'm catching on fast, aren't I?" said the pope with a grin.

"You are indeed, Your Holiness," said Guido solicitously. "Now I'm going to point to individual notes, and I'd like you to sing the note I'm pointing to."

As he pointed to E, then up to A, then G, then A again, then on up to B and C, the pope sang the correct pitches without difficulty.

"This is fun!" exclaimed the pope to his canons. "You should try this."

They all nodded nervously and smiled.

"Now you're ready to sing the actual notes of the first two lines of *Te Deum laudamus*," said Guido, saying a silent prayer that his lesson had actually sunk in. Returning to the page in the chant book, and pointing slowly at each note in succession, Guido led the pope in singing the pitches. A few times John had to listen to Guido for guidance ("Oh, right!" he then exclaimed), but he kept going and successfully navigated the two lines of music.

"And now all we do is add the words," said Guido, next leading the pope in singing the pitches with their proper words and rhythms.

This time the pontiff sang with even more confidence. "Can I try it by myself?" asked Pope John excitedly.

"If you'd like," answered Guido guardedly as he exchanged another look with Petro.

Taking a deep breath, proceeding slowly and deliberately, with his eyes fixed doggedly on the chant book page, the pope sang:

Te Deum laudamus: te Dominum confitemur.
Te aeternum Patrem omnis terra veneratur.

When he was finished, he looked up expectantly at Guido, whose face was beaming.

"That was exactly right, Your Holiness!"

"I did it!" crowed the pope. "Your method works like a charm."

"And yet to learn this using the old ways, without written music, would have taken you weeks or months or even years."

"Guido, you're a bloody genius!" exclaimed the pope. "We must have you here in Rome. You must train all of our clergy and our singers. This is the seat of the Church, and the music here must be the very best."

Taken aback, Guido responded tentatively, "I . . . I would be honored, Your Holiness."

"Then stay. You already have your apartment in the Lateran Palace. I'll supply you with everything you need for your work."

"Your Holiness, please allow me a night of prayerful consideration," asked Guido.

"Of course, of course. I know this is all very sudden. But you belong here at the center of things," added the pope, beckoning to the patiently waiting emissary who had escorted the visitors from the palace.

"Thank you, Your Holiness," said Guido, sensing that the papal audience was ending. He bowed reverentially and backed down the steps of the throne, rejoining his two comrades.

As they were led back across the plaza, Dom Petro turned to

Guido and whispered with a smile, "Like I said: a man of great discernment."

Although he had again wrapped his nose and mouth in a scarf before venturing outdoors, Guido was coughing violently by the time he returned to his Lateran Palace room. He skipped the evening meal, preferring not to leave his chambers but also seeing the advantage of fasting as he weighed his momentous decision.

Agonizing over the pope's proposal, Guido stayed awake far into the night, pacing the room and praying—amid sporadic coughing—for heavenly guidance. For a servant of the Church, a summons to Rome was the ultimate seal of approval. If his methods were already spreading across Italy thanks to Bishop Theodaldus's support, he could only imagine what greater circulation they would receive with the sponsorship of the pope. A soft feather mattress and bountiful meals could be very easy to accustom himself to. And he had to admit that in recent years he had been increasingly unhappy with life at the cathedral.

But Guido also knew that he owed much of his success to Theodaldus and hated the idea of deserting the benevolent bishop without warning. Arezzo's new Church of St. Donatus was nearing completion, and it was his duty to prepare the music for its special service of dedication. His health would clearly suffer if he remained in Rome, perhaps irreparably. The little earthenware chalice in his cupboard at the rectory was silently calling him back. And Rome was even further than Arezzo from Pomposa and Brother Michael.

Finally Guido collapsed on the bed and fell into a troubled slumber. When he awoke the next morning, he felt even sicker, with racking coughs tearing through his entire body. If he needed a sign from above, apparently this was it. His health simply could not endure Rome's poisonous summer vapors. Sending word that he needed to speak briefly to Pope John, he rested in hopes of regaining his strength for the return journey to Arezzo. In a few hours, another emissary arrived to take him to the pope.

John XIX was being fitted for new vestments in his palace suite but saw nothing amiss in bringing Guido into the room amid the swarm of tailors and attendants. The monk started to kiss John's ring again, but the pope waved him off.

"No need for that," laughed the pontiff. "I hope you're here to tell me you're staying in Rome."

With a sigh, and after clearing his throat in hopes of forestalling a cough, Guido offered his prepared answer. "Alas, Your Holiness, I would be of little use to you in my present condition. The foul air from the swamps has infected my lungs, and I could not expect to regain my health as long as the weather here remains warm. But I will plan to return this winter when conditions will be more conducive." With that, he lapsed into another coughing fit.

Not accustomed to being turned down, the pope scowled. But as the coughing continued, he shrugged and said, "It will be better for you, and for us too, if you stay healthy. But promise you will come back as soon as the weather turns cold."

"I will do all within my power," answered Guido, gasping

to catch his breath. "Thank you for your confidence in my methods."

"The cape needs to be shorter—I'm practically tripping over it," said Pope John to one of the tailors, so Guido bowed deferentially and slipped away.

After a few more days, Guido felt hopeful that he could withstand the return journey, so he set out with Dom Petro and Abbot Grimaldus for Rieti. The more he thought about his decision, the more Guido felt sure it was the right one. To remain in Rome permanently would place him under constant obligation to humble himself before the Church's ultimate earthly authority—a mercurial man whose character scarcely merited such respect. Whatever the woes Guido had suffered in Arezzo, at least Theodaldus was an honorable bishop who demanded no such subjugation. And humility had never been Guido's strong point.

Chapter Fifteen

AN UNEXPECTED INVITATION

R etracing their earlier journey, Guido and his companions enjoyed returning to San Cataldo and San Pietro, and both abbeys welcomed them back warmly. But Guido was still battling the ailment he had developed in Rome and was aching with fatigue by the time they arrived at both destinations. There was even talk in Perugia of delaying their departure for Arezzo to allow the convalescent monk more time to recover, but it was Guido himself who insisted they push on, as he was eager to get back to familiar surroundings.

Before they reached Arezzo, Abbot Grimaldus took his leave of the two others to return to his own abbey at Badicroce. As they parted ways, Guido reached into his satchel, found his copy of the chant book, and presented it to the abbot, who promised that Badicroce's cantor would soon be adopting its methods.

Riding together the remaining distance, tired from the extended journey, Guido and Dom Petro were uncharacteristically silent. Letting his mind settle into a zone of contemplation,

Guido found himself replaying the pleasant memory of his lesson with Pope John.

He was able to learn the tones of the scale readily enough by following the neumes on the staff, thought Guido. *But he might have grasped them even more quickly if I could have offered him something less theoretical than just a notated scale.*

Humming a scale softly to himself, he idly wondered: *Instead of an abstract sequence, what if there was a chant melody where the first notes of each new phrase formed an ascending scale? But the chant's words would have to be a hymn with the right number of phrases, and ideally with just one strophe.*

Clip-clopping down the path, he mentally cycled through a few likely hymn texts, counting the number of phrases. They were all too long, and eventually Guido stopped even trying to consciously think of more options. But then, out of nowhere, the words of the old hymn to St. John the Baptist popped into his head:

Ut queant laxis
Resonare fibris
Mira gestorum
Famuli tuorum,
Solve polluti
Labii reatum,
Sancte Johannes

With the warbling of birds and the chirping of crickets lulling him into a daze, he found himself casually improvising a melody to the hymn's words, starting with the initial syllable "Ut" on the melody's lowest note. At the end of that phrase, he started a new phrase on the next highest scale tone, beginning with the syllable "re-" of *resonare*. The ensuing phrase started naturally on the next scale degree with "mi-" of *mira*, followed by the fourth on "fa-" of *famuli*, the fifth on "sol-" of *solve*, and the sixth on "la-" of *labii*. Still singing offhandedly, he improvised a finishing phrase to wrap things up on the words *Sancte Johannes*—and then wondered laughingly if he could even remember the tune he had just made up.

But starting again from the beginning, still singing softly but now with more conscious intent, he found himself repeating his new melody phrase by phrase. The scale gracefully unfolded upward step by step as each new phrase began on the next higher scale note: *ut, re, mi, fa, sol, la.*

I must write this down when we get back to Arezzo, thought Guido. *Maybe I'll try it out with my choirboys.*

Abruptly, Petro's voice intruded on his reverie. "So you'll be leaving us soon to return to Rome."

"Only if I feel well enough to travel this winter," said Guido, reluctantly emerging from his productive daydream as the tune continued to run through his head. "And I would only remain there until spring. My health couldn't withstand another onslaught of the summer vapors."

"I know Bishop Theodaldus would be sorry to lose you, even temporarily."

"If it weren't for him, you know I'd gladly leave the cathedral tomorrow," sighed Guido. "I'm so tired of the squabbling and corruption of the priests—except for you, of course, and a few others. And the endless progression of untutored boys year after year has worn me down. Our visits to San Cataldo and San Pietro made me realize how much I miss the cloister."

"But weren't you terribly unhappy in Pomposa?" asked Petro delicately.

By now the new John the Baptist tune had retreated to some far corner of Guido's mind. With a sigh of resignation, he said, "It's discouraging, when we try to follow Christ, how we always end up fighting with each other. The gospel of peace, indeed."

They rode the rest of the way to Arezzo in silence.

The first thing Guido did after returning to his room in the rectory was to peek into his cupboard. He let out a sigh of relief, reassured to see that his father's chalice was still resting intact on the shelf.

Early the next morning, Bishop Theodaldus summoned Guido and Petro for a full report on their journey.

"Brother Guido literally taught the pope to learn how to sing a new hymn from his chant book," said Petro admiringly.

"And thanks to my lesson, he sang it perfectly," said Guido, daring to brag a bit.

"After that," added Petro, "His Holiness wanted him to stay in Rome and take over the music training there immediately."

"But . . . apparently you didn't," said the bishop, clearly curious as to why.

"The hot, swampy climate was affecting my health," said Guido, stifling a cough. "In fact, I still haven't fully recovered.

And I knew I needed to return here for the dedication of St. Donatus Church. But I told the pope I would try to return temporarily this winter. With your permission, of course."

"Obviously the Holy See would take priority," said Theodaldus. "In any case, I'm glad the visit was a success. But Guido, as it happens, I believe you have another option."

"What do you mean?" asked Guido, genuinely puzzled.

"Two days ago, I received a visitor who came here expressly to see you. Of course, he had no way of knowing you'd been called to Rome. He had given up on waiting for you and was planning to leave tomorrow, but by the grace of God, here you are, just in time."

"Who might this be?" asked Guido.

Noticing the rectory's household servant passing along the corridor, the bishop rose and called for him. "Oliverio, please summon our visitor from the guest quarters."

Returning to the conversation, Theodaldus said, "I'll tell you this much. It's someone you know."

Guido's head was spinning. Who could have come to visit him? Much as he tried to stifle his hopes, he couldn't help wondering if it could be Brother Michael. Would he finally see his friend again?

As Guido sat tensely, Dom Petro offered various idle speculations, despite not having the slightest clue about the mystery. After what seemed like hours but was probably just a few minutes, approaching footsteps were finally heard.

"Guido, how wonderful to see you!" The visitor entering the room was indeed from Pomposa, but he was not the man Guido had most hoped to see. His special visitor was the abbot who shared his name.

"Dom Guido, what a surprise," said the monk as he rose in greeting, struggling to hide his disappointment. "Whatever could have brought you here?"

"Our little corner of the world in Pomposa is intentionally set apart from society, as you know very well," said the abbot. "But even there, from time to time we receive visitors who bring us word of what is going on at other abbeys and churches."

Guido listened without any idea where this train of thought might be leading.

"Lately, we've heard from several visitors about a wonderful new method that is revolutionizing the training of choirs in cathedrals and other monasteries, both here in Arezzo and in other places that have adopted it."

But that could only mean my *method,* thought Guido, more confused than ever.

Taking a deep breath, the abbot went on. "Brother Guido, I made a terrible mistake when I sent you away from Pomposa. In you we had a pearl of great price, and we let it slip through our fingers."

Worse than that, you flung it away, thought Guido, still resentful.

"I have come to invite you to return to Pomposa as our cantor, our singing master."

"But Brother Anselmo . . . ?" asked Guido.

"Brother Anselmo has gone to his reward," said Dom Guido calmly.

Guido bowed his head. "May he rest in eternal peace."

"Amen." Resuming after a moment of silence, the abbot said, "I speak to you now as one monk to another. With all due respect to the reverend bishop"—here Dom Guido gave a deferential nod to Theodaldus—"I know that you were raised to live a life of meditation and contemplation. What we can offer you, no cathedral can provide, even one as magnificent as this."

"I must confess, at times I've had these same thoughts myself," admitted Guido.

"Then come back. We can at least atone for our error in sending you away."

Guido's heart warmed at this long-delayed reconciliation with his spiritual father. And the thought of a reunion with Brother Michael was almost enough to make him accept the proposal on the spot. But he needed to make sure the abbot understood the full implications of his offer.

"If I were to return," cautioned Guido, "it would require much labor in the scriptorium to copy my writings and chant book."

"I am fully prepared to provide you with the necessary resources," promised the abbot. "And we already possess a copy of your most excellent chant book, which one of the monks is already engaged in copying."

The chant book that started out as a stack of parchment pages under Michael's blanket and earned both of us forty days and nights of imprisonment, thought Guido ruefully. But despite the irony of the abbot's offer, the monk was sorely tempted by the proposition.

Conscious of his obligations to Theodaldus, Guido replied in measured tones, "I am most appreciative of your kind proposal, and I promise to give it my most thoughtful consideration. But I've just returned from Rome, where the pope wishes me to take on the training of his choirs this winter. Here in November, I must lead the special music for the dedication of our new Church of St. Donatus. And I owe too much loyalty and reverence to our esteemed bishop here in Arezzo to ever leave the cathedral without at least choosing a successor and thoroughly preparing him to take my place."

"I understand," said the abbot, inwardly relieved—after all the controversy with Guido at Pomposa—that at least the monk hadn't spurned the offer outright.

"Also, I became quite ill in Rome, so in any case I am in no condition to do any further traveling until I regain my health."

"I'm sorry to hear of that," said the abbot. "I pray for your full and speedy recovery."

"Thank you, and thank you again for inviting me back to the abbey," replied Guido. "I shall hope one day to rejoin you there, but at present I can make no more definite commitment."

"I shall hope that day comes," said the abbot, sensing that the interview was ending. "May God bless you."

As he turned to leave, Guido stopped him. "Dom Guido," he said hesitantly. "Might I ask you to please convey my warmest greetings to my musical accomplice, Brother Michael?"

"Oh, I almost forgot," said the abbot, reaching into a pocket of his cassock for a slim, sealed parchment scroll. "Brother

Michael asked me to give you this. And yes, of course I'll give him your greetings."

Turning again to leave, the abbot said, "Bishop Theodaldus, thank you for your generous hospitality. I fear we have overstayed our welcome, and I know I have deserted my post for far too long, so my party will leave within the hour for Pomposa. We are immensely grateful for our warm reception here."

"Of course," said Theodaldus, ushering him out. "Godspeed on your journey." Then he politely dismissed Dom Petro and returned to Guido. "I know you have much to consider," he said. "Please take all the time you need to make your decision. I will support you on whatever path you choose."

"As you have always supported me," said Guido with considerable emotion. "My first loyalty remains with you."

Guido's heart was racing as he returned to his room in the rectory, tightly clutching the scroll from Michael. With trembling fingers, he broke the seal, unrolled the parchment page, and read his friend's letter.

To the most blessed and beloved Brother Guido, from Michael, stifled by the opposition of the resentful.

When you came to bid me farewell before leaving for Arezzo, I had no inkling that it had been the abbot's deliberate decision to separate us. But that soon became abundantly clear, for quickly all traces of your existence were erased from the abbey.

I alone remained, to be regarded as an unpleasant, inescapable reminder of the trouble that you are unfairly blamed for causing.

For that reason, I have been effectively exiled within the monastery walls. No one ever speaks to me, or even looks me in the eye. Circatores—wandering spies—track my every move. To deprive me of contact with my fellows, I am assigned arduous labor that was formerly assigned to servants—carrying heavy burdens, making repairs, emptying chamber pots. No matter how many new monks are added to the brotherhood of the abbey, my position in the hierarchy remains at the very bottom, whether in processions, at meals, or in chapter meetings. Although my door remains unlocked, I am now obliged to dwell alone in the same tiny cell where I was imprisoned for forty days and nights by the onerous decree of Bishop Cunibert.

Despite these tribulations, I regret nothing. Our friendship has been the one bright ray of light in my entire earthly existence, and my present sufferings will never outweigh the joy we found in spiritual communion. The only thing that sustains me from day to day is the fervent hope that someday we may be reunited—if not on earth, then surely in paradise.

Guido was frantic with anxiety. *Surely the letter must have been written before Dom Guido decided to invite me back to Pomposa,* he thought distractedly. For a moment he was hopeful; perhaps Michael's condition had already improved, now that the abbey was no longer erasing all signs of Guido's existence and in fact was even making a copy of his chant book. But then he realized that because of Michael's forced isolation, the beleaguered monk might be the last to know of the abbot's change in attitude.

Slowly rereading the letter that he had raced through the first time, Guido became more and more agitated. *I must send a response as soon as possible*, he said to himself, trying to think clearly. He rummaged around for a blank sheet of parchment, then grabbed his quill so violently that he accidentally broke it. Seated on the bench, he tried to think what to write, but his thoughts were a jumble. Suddenly, with the parchment still blank and the quill unsharpened, he began to wonder how he might get the eventual letter delivered.

Maybe Dom Guido hasn't yet left for Pomposa, he thought. *I could ask him to wait while I write to Michael.*

Rushing out of his room, Guido literally ran through the rectory and out into the courtyard, past the nearly completed Church of St. Donatus beside the main cathedral, and finally reached the stables. Breathlessly, he found the stable boy and asked, "Has Dom Guido already left with his party for Pomposa?"

"Why yes, they left a while ago," said the boy, busily filling a horse's feedbag.

"Could I take a horse and try to catch up with him?"

"Oh, no, we only have these two, and they're both old and slow," the boy explained. "Neither one would ever make it past the next town, especially with a rider in a hurry."

For a moment Guido stood panting in frustration. Then he

was overtaken with a sudden chill, and as he began shivering, his coughing resumed with a vengeance. Within moments he was doubled over in pain.

"Reverend brother, you're not well. Let me help you back inside."

With Guido holding onto one of the boy's arms for dear life, the faltering monk was led back to his room in the rectory. The Roman contagion, never banished completely, now racked Guido's body from head to toe. Collapsing in agony on his mattress, he fell into a state of feverish delirium, tortured by thoughts of Michael's suffering and of his own irreconcilable choices.

The stable boy alerted Oliverio, who made sure that the ailing monk was properly cared for, and both Bishop Theodaldus and Dom Petro came to visit him at least once a day. Taking advantage of his fellow clerics' inevitable sympathy for a sick colleague, Petro quietly negotiated a reduction of hostilities, pledging that he would make sure Guido attended to his own affairs and didn't meddle in theirs, as long as they agreed to treat him with at least basic cordiality. The priests and canons agreed readily enough to what increasingly appeared to be a moot point. Few expected Guido to recover.

Chapter Sixteen

A LETTER TO MICHAEL

Unbeknownst to Guido, Pope John XIX was touting the monk's methods to every cleric visiting the Holy See as well as keeping his scribes busy producing copies of Guido's books for even wider dissemination. The recognition from Brother Rizardo at San Cataldo was merely a token of Guido's growing fame as it spread up and down the Italian peninsula.

But the thought of fame was the last thing in Guido's fevered brain as he lay writhing in agony for weeks on end. There was no reprieve from the coughing, aching, and shivering. Music ran through his head constantly, but it was all harshly discordant and shrill. Every time he began to regain an awareness of his surroundings, his mind was flooded with anxious thoughts. Should he go back to Rome? Should he return to Pomposa? Should he stay at Arezzo? Was Brother Michael still suffering? Wrestling in vain with these insoluble quandaries, he would again relapse into barely conscious confusion.

After dark one evening, as a flickering candle threw shadows against the wall and Guido lay motionless on his mattress, the harsh cacophony in his head gradually faded to a merciful silence. For almost an hour he lay somewhere between wakefulness and sleep. Then out of the void, somewhere in his mind arose a simple melody. What was it? With his eyes closed, Guido tried his best to focus. He could hear the tune now as it progressed from phrase to phrase, gradually restarting higher and higher.

Suddenly his eyes popped open and he sat up in bed. The tune running through his mind was the melody he had improvised for *Ut queant laxis* on the road from Perugia to Arezzo. He had completely forgotten the whole idea of a hymn with phrases beginning on each successive tone of an ascending scale, much less the melody itself. But now he heard it clearly in his head, and so he began singing softly:

> *Ut queant laxis*
> *Resonare fibris*
> *Mira gestorum*
> *Famuli tuorum,*
> *Solve polluti*
> *Labii reatum,*
> *Sancte Johannes*

I must write this down, he thought urgently. Getting out of bed for the first time in weeks, he moved to the table, where his quill and inkhorn lay neglected alongside blank sheets of parchment. By the dim candlelight, humming softly as he worked,

Guido drew his four-line staves, wrote in the neumes for the melody, and added the words under the appropriate notes.

When he was finished, he gazed at the page and heaved a sigh. And then he returned to his mattress and enjoyed his first completely restful night's sleep since his trip to Rome.

The next morning, as Canon Francesco was preparing as usual to begin the day's lesson with the boys' choir, he was startled when Guido unexpectedly entered the room, looking surprisingly rested after his long illness. The monk was clutching a freshly inscribed sheet of parchment.

"Look at this, Francesco!" Guido exclaimed, setting the sheet in front of his assistant. Pointing to the music as he chanted, he sang his new setting of *Ut queant laxis*.

"Do you see how each phrase begins on the next higher note of the scale?" he asked eagerly. "C is *ut*, D is *re*, E is *mi*, F is *fa*, G is *sol*, and A is *la*!"

"Yes, I see, Brother Guido!" said Francesco, catching on quickly.

"Boys, gather round," said Guido with renewed authority. "I have a new hymn for you to learn!"

Once the boys had thoroughly mastered his latest creation, Guido explained its unique usefulness. "Now, when you start learning a new chant and need to find the first note, just remember the *Ut queant laxis* phrase that begins with that same tone of the scale. And then do the same for each of the other notes, relating them back to the first note of the appropriate *Ut queant laxis* phrase. As long as you've learned the six scale notes—*ut, re, mi, fa, sol, la*—reading a new chant at sight should be easy. Here, let's try it," continued Guido, barely able to contain his excitement. "Open your chant books to a hymn you haven't learned yet. Let's try *Vita sanctorum via.*"

Sure enough, as the boys identified the scale notes in the unfamiliar chant and tried to find the pitches of its melody, they simply started humming the corresponding phrase of *Ut queant laxis* and were readily able to orient themselves to the proper pattern. In less than a half hour, they were all singing *Vita sanctorum via* with complete confidence.

"It works in reverse too," said Guido. "If I sing you an unfamiliar chant, and you want to write it down, just relate the notes you hear to the beginning notes of the *Ut queant laxis* phrases. Francesco, let's show them."

His assistant was a bit worried about being put on the spot, but after inscribing a blank four-line staff on the back of Guido's *Ut queant laxis* sheet, he listened intently while his mentor improvised a brief melody. Sounding each note individually, Francesco then determined which starting syllable it matched and soon had the whole phrase correctly notated.

One precocious boy even put two and two together and sang an ascending scale on the initial syllables of the six phrases: *ut, re, mi, fa, sol, la.*

"Exactly!" shouted Guido. "A whole new addition to my method!"

Guido's recovery was incomplete—he still tired quickly and in fact never regained the robust health he had enjoyed before going to Rome. But he was gradually able to resume his cathedral responsibilities, just in time to oversee musical preparations for the special service to dedicate the new Church of St. Donatus. Thanks to Dom Petro's intervention, the priests and canons now treated him civilly. And when Petro confessed his behind-the-scenes efforts to Guido, the easily exhausted monk was only too willing to agree that henceforth he would focus on his own duties and leave clerical misbehavior for others to address—or not.

The pedagogical success of *Ut queant laxis* even inspired Guido to begin writing a new treatise—*Ad invendiendum ignotum cantum* (*Figuring out an unknown chant*)—to outline his most recent ideas. After explaining how to use *Ut queant laxis* as a way of learning to sing unfamiliar chant melodies, he revisited many of the ideas from the early chapters of his *Micrologus*, summarizing his latest theoretical thinking. But as soon as the document was finished, he knew that he could no longer postpone making key decisions about his future.

Finally, on a warm fall day, he took a walk down a nearby path along the mountains. Slowly but methodically, he was able to weigh his conflicting options and draw the only possible conclusions. That evening, seated at the table in his room, Guido wrote two letters. The first was to the abbot in Pomposa.

To the most reverend abbot, Dom Guido, my spiritual father, from Guido, a monk in service at the Cathedral of St. Maria and St. Stefano.

Again I sincerely thank you for most considerately visiting me in Arezzo and for generously inviting me to return to the abbey of Pomposa.

The pope (*Even this pope,* thought Guido as he wrote) *is the ruler of our Holy Church. As a servant of the Church, I owe him my obedience. When the weather begins to turn cool, I will return to Rome at his command, although to protect my health, I will only stay through the winter.*

As a musician, I owe so much to Bishop Theodaldus. It was he who first endorsed my teaching methods and who encouraged me to write my treatises and compile my chant book. If it were not for his efforts to promote my work, you would never have known of my success here and thus would never have invited me to return to Pomposa. Ties of affection and friendship draw me back to the monastery, but because of the debt of gratitude that I owe to Theodaldus, I will serve him as long as he wishes for me to remain at the cathedral. If and when those circumstances change, I will most gratefully return to Pomposa.

In the meantime, I humbly ask of you a favor. Brother Michael, for whom I served as custos animi—*guardian of the soul— during his term as a novice, has suffered greatly on my account. If my sins against the brotherhood have been forgiven to so great an extent that I have been invited to come back to Pomposa as cantor, surely his lesser infractions deserve equal pardon. I respectfully implore you to restore him to full communion in the abbey.*

After becoming increasingly distressed in rereading the scroll that Michael had sent him, Guido started a second letter—knowing that he could end it on a positive note by appending his short treatise on how to use *Ut queant laxis.*

To the most blessed and amiable Brother Michael, from Guido, discouraged and encumbered on his tortuous path.

Either the times are difficult or the heavenly intention is unclear; for all too frequently, truth is crushed by falsehood and compassion by ill will, even within our brotherhood.

Why should the assembled Philistines punish the iniquity of Israel, unless—when something happens according to our desires—we are so pleased about it that we credit our own efforts and invite condemnation? Our work is indeed good, as long as we ascribe everything we do to our Creator.

Therefore you see that I am exiled from you to a faraway country, and you are stifled by the retaliation of the spiteful.

Here Guido came to the end of the letter's first parchment sheet, so he set it aside and continued on a new one.

Your letter filled me with intense sorrow, especially inasmuch as it is I who caused your sufferings. The harmonious communion of our souls has brought much contentment to my earthly existence, and I grieve daily that my actions have brought upon you such dire tribulations.

On the remainder of this page, Guido drew staffs and wrote out the melody—without the words—for the chant *Ubi caritas*, the first hymn he had ever notated for Michael. He knew that his friend would recognize the music and would immediately recall the text.

Where charity and love are, God is there.
Love of Christ has gathered us into one.
Let us rejoice in Him and be glad.
Let us fear, and let us love the living God.
And from a sincere heart let us love one another.
Where charity and love are, God is there.
Therefore, whenever we are gathered as one:
Lest we be divided in mind, let us beware.
Let malicious quarrels stop, let controversy cease.
And in the midst of us be Christ our God.
Where charity and love are, God is there.
Together also with the blessed may we see
Thy face in glory, O Christ our God:
The joy that is immense and good,
Through infinite ages without end. Amen.

Much later, when giving Guido's letter to a scribe for copying so that the *Ut queant laxis* treatise could be widely read, Michael withheld this second page; he kept it with him for the rest of his life. Meanwhile, after Guido had completed the second page, he began a new parchment sheet, and the first and remaining pages of his letter were eventually copied and preserved.

Inspired by divine love, I have shared the gifts I have unde-servedly received from God, not only with you but also with others who might profit from them. Having helped so many to learn with the greatest ease the chants that I and everyone before me learned with the greatest difficulty, I can only hope that those who so profited will reward us by offering prayers for our salvation. For if those who were scarcely able to acquire an imperfect knowledge of singing from their teachers in ten years still pray to God on their teachers' behalf, what do you think will be done for us who now produce a perfect singer in only one year, or at most two? Or if despicable humanity turns out to be ungrateful as usual, surely God will reward our efforts? Like the apostle Paul, I can only say, "I have fought the good fight, I have finished the race, I have kept the faith. Henceforth, there is laid up for me a crown of righteousness." Now that fair weather is returning after a host of storms, there should be smooth sailing ahead.

But since unfortunately you are still in confinement, I write to apprise you of recent events. Pope John, having learned of our cathedral's success in using my chant book to train choirboys to learn chants they had never before heard, sent three emissaries to summon me. So I journeyed to Rome with Dom Grimaldus, an esteemed abbot, and the most learned Dom Petro, prefect of the canons at Arezzo's cathedral. The pope was delighted to welcome me and engaged me in conversation, asking me many questions. He greatly marveled at our chant book, and after I introduced him to the principles of notation, he did not get up from his throne until, at his insistence, he had learned the beginning of a chant that he had never before heard. Then he knew from his own experience what he had doubted in others.

I could not remain long in Rome because I quickly fell ill, succumbing to the summer heat and swampy vapors so toxic to a native of the mountains like me. But I agreed to return this winter to train his clergy in my methods. Later I visited Dom Guido, our abbot in Pomposa and my spiritual father, who has belatedly realized the value of our chant book, and who apologized for having sided with our opponents. He invited me to return to Pomposa, pointing out that for a monk, a monastery is a more suitable atmosphere than a cathedral.

By the grace of God, I hope to be able to accede to the abbot's wishes, particularly because of the simony and other corrupt practices that are so rife among the cathedral clergy. But for the present I must continue to fulfill my obligations to my patron, the reverend bishop, and so our reunion, for which I pray daily, must be further postponed.

In hopes that your torments will soon be allayed, and in light of your close involvement in my musical efforts, I am providing the pages that follow, outlining a new method for learning an unfamiliar chant.

At that point Guido attached the pages of *Ad invendiendum ignotum cantum*, the short treatise he had written about using *Ut queant laxis*.

The next day, Guido rolled up the pages of both letters into scrolls—Dom Guido's slim, Michael's quite hefty—and securely sealed each with wax. Then he brought them to Bishop Theodaldus, requesting that he ask any visitors to Arezzo whether they might be traveling in the direction of Pomposa. The bishop readily agreed, but no potential couriers appeared for many weeks, and the two scrolls continued to rest undelivered on top of the bishop's pine cabinet.

Meanwhile, autumn had arrived, and the trees were soon clothed in rich hues of yellow, orange, and red. On a Sunday in mid-November, Guido led the music for the special service dedicating the beautiful new Church of St. Donatus. The following week, having delayed as long as possible, he finally began planning his return journey to the court of Pope John XIX in hopes of reaching Rome before the first snowfall. Again he prepared Canon Francesco to assume his duties in his absence. Once he had settled on a late November date for his departure, Guido sought out Bishop Theodaldus to obtain his blessing.

Entering the bishop's chamber, Guido instinctively glanced at the cabinet.

"My scrolls are gone!" he exclaimed. "Has someone come along to deliver them?"

"Yes, a messenger from Rome arrived late yesterday and left this morning," said the bishop. "He plans to visit every monastery, convent, and cathedral from here to Venice, so he agreed to carry your letters to Pomposa."

"Thanks be to God," said Guido. "But what errand could be taking him to so many places of devotion?"

"He is notifying the Church across Italy that Pope John has died."

Chapter Seventeen

IN THE PALM OF HIS HAND

Guido said a prayer for the soul of Pope John. He knew nothing of how much the pope had done to spread his fame across Italy and even beyond. All he knew was that John's death relieved him of the obligation of returning to Rome—an expedition he had been privately dreading.

So once again his principal allegiance was to Bishop Theodaldus, and now his duties were even more extensive, with Masses and canonical hours to be led at both the original Cathedral of St. Maria and St. Stefano and the new adjacent Church of St. Donatus. Fortunately, Canon Francesco had developed into an invaluable assistant, so Guido was able to delegate many of his responsibilities to the musician he was grooming to succeed him. Much of Guido's energy was still devoted to overseeing the scribes copying his writings and chant book, but this year's especially perceptive and inquisitive cohort of choirboys lifted his spirits and kept him on his toes.

On the wall of the music room, Guido had mounted a large sheet of felt bearing a blank four-line staff. Since felt adheres to felt, he then cut two small pieces, inscribing a C-clef sign on one and a neume on the other. Using these accessories, he enjoyed playing a game with the boys. After sounding a C on the monochord, he would place the clef at the beginning of a line and position the neume on a line or space, then ask the young choristers to sing the resulting note. Moving the clef and neume to different positions, he continued the exercise to other notes on the staff. At first the boys found the game challenging, but in time their responses became both speedy and accurate.

The following spring, the weather stayed cool far later than usual. Finally, one morning in May, the temperature was suddenly much warmer. Guido let a balmy breeze waft through the music room window, but that wasn't enough for the restless boys.

"Can we practice our music outside?" said one of the boys plaintively.

"Yes! Yes!" shouted the others.

Guido had never before conducted an al fresco music rehearsal, but the day was sunny, the ground was dry, and the boys had been working hard all year. The cluttered construction site around the new church had finally been cleared, so there was a conveniently open area right outside the school.

"All right," said Guido, prompting loud cheers. "Bring your chant books and line up in order."

The boys did as they were told, and soon the procession marched outside, the choristers resuming their positions under the shade of an ancient beech tree. Making use of the chant books, Guido ran through the music the boys would be singing for upcoming services. They had learned everything so well that he finished reviewing their music well before the scheduled end of his rehearsal.

"This is when I'd usually have you play the sing-the-note game," said Guido, "but we'll have to go back inside for that."

"No! No!" moaned the boys, enjoying the rare opportunity to sing in the open air.

"All right, let's see," said Guido, doing his best to improvise. For a few moments he stared intently at the ground. Then he suddenly looked at the palm of his left hand. "How about this?" he asked, thinking aloud.

Humming a low pitch, he said, "This is a G."

As the boys hummed the note back, Guido held out his left palm to face them.

"On my hand, let's say that this is G"—with his right forefinger, he indicated the tip of his left thumb—"this is A" (the upper thumb joint), "and this is B" (the lower thumb joint).

That was as far as he had gotten with his spur-of-the-moment idea, but he at least needed to complete more of the scale. Impulsively moving from the lower thumb joint to the next closest joint, he continued, "This is C" (the lowest forefinger joint), "this is D" (the lowest middle-finger joint), "and this is E" (the lowest fourth-finger joint).

As much to make sure he remembered his hastily devised scheme himself as to confirm the boys' comprehension, he asked them to say the letter names as he pointed, in order, to the appropriate spots on his left hand.

"G, A, B, C, D, E," they all repeated as he moved down the thumb and across the base of the fingers.

"Very good," said Guido. "Do you still remember the G that you hummed?"

They did, and they all hummed it again.

"Here we go," said Guido. "Sing this note." With an exaggerated gesture, he pressed his right forefinger onto the bottom joint of his left middle finger. A few stray pitches were heard, but most of the boys sang a D.

"Excellent!" said Guido. Next he pointed to the lower joint of his left thumb. All the boys knew to sing a lower pitch, and nearly all of them actually sang the correct one—B.

Continuing to quiz the boys on the notes of this scale, Guido kept his right forefinger busy tapping on the appropriate finger joints. As soon as the choristers were singing all the notes perfectly, he divided them in half, assigning one group to follow his right forefinger and the other his right thumb. When he then pointed to G and D, the boys cheerily hummed the harmonious perfect fifth.

On a whim, Guido moved his right thumb and forefinger each inward one position, and the boys now sang A and C. Repositioning both the higher and lower voice parts onto his lower thumb joint led them to a lovely unison on B. Then he reversed the process, but moving one voice at a time—the lower voice to A, then the upper voice to C, then the upper to D, the lower to G, and finally the upper back down through C to B. After holding that final concord till they ran out of breath, the boys collapsed in laughter.

"We should sing like this in church!" screamed one of the boys.

Not a bad suggestion, thought Guido, recalling that near the end of his own *Micrologus* he had explored this same idea of oblique and contrary motion between voices. At the very least, among the cohort of boys who would help shape the next generation's music at the cathedral, he had planted a seed: independent movement of voice parts.

Back in his room that evening, Guido gazed at his left hand and remembered the morning's impromptu exercise. *I barely used much of my hand*, he thought. *I wonder how much further up the scale I could go?*

Humming in his own baritone register, Guido sounded the low G as he touched the tip of his left thumb, then retraced his way up the scale through A, B, C, D, and E as he touched the appropriate joints, ending on the lower joint of his fourth finger—just as he had shown the boys. Those six notes were an exact transposition of the *ut re mi fa sol la* notes of his *Ut queant laxis*. But this time he kept going to the lower joint of his pinkie finger for F and then up that finger to the middle joint (G) and upper joint (A), with G and A now starting a new scale an octave above the original one. That put B at the tip of the pinkie; thus far he'd traced a circular pattern down from the tip of the thumb across the lower finger joints and up the pinkie, so he continued the circle across the tips of the fourth and middle fingers as C and D.

Turning the circle into a spiral, he continued to the tip of the forefinger for E, then down that finger to its upper and middle joints as F and G. Since the lower forefinger joint had long since been assigned, he kept spiraling across to the right for the middle joints of the third finger (A) and fourth finger (B), then proceeded up and back left to the fourth and third fingers' upper joints (C and D).

Those last five joint positions (G, A, B, C, D) almost completed another *ut re mi fa sol la* pattern, two octaves above the original one—except the last note was missing. Determined to finish the sequence, he rotated his wrist and touched the back of his hand: E!

Making sure he wouldn't forget the whole spiral of hand positions, Guido took out a fresh sheet of parchment, placed his left hand on it with the palm face up, and traced the outline. After writing all the notes' letter names in the appropriate places, he drew curving lines in different ink colors to show the interlocking *ut re mi fa sol la* patterns.

Within a few days, Guido had produced enough copies of his hand diagram to give one to each member of his boys' and men's choirs. Once they had memorized the spiral pattern, he quizzed them daily by pointing to the different fingertips and joints of his hand as a prompt for singing specific pitches. For choristers at Arezzo, "Guido's Hand" became a useful addition to their musical education.

As months and then years elapsed, Guido waited in vain for some response to his letters to Pomposa. He constantly worried that the messenger had for some reason failed to deliver them—perhaps he had been waylaid by robbers or had lost the scrolls while fording a river, or had ended up taking an alternate route that bypassed Pomposa. Of course, Guido had no idea how many different monasteries, convents, and cathedrals the messenger had intended to visit between Arezzo and Pomposa or how many months those errands might have required. And perhaps the letters had indeed been delivered and replies dispatched but some misfortune had befallen the return messenger. Endless speculations swirled in Guido's mind, but he knew of no way to lift the cloud of uncertainty.

Most of all, he worried about Brother Michael. Logic would suggest that if his own reputation at Pomposa had taken a dramatic turn for the better, surely there was no reason for further animosity toward his erstwhile confederate. But with no more recent communication to go on, Guido found himself repeatedly rereading his letter from Michael and empathizing anew with his friend's suffering.

Having pledged his loyalty to Bishop Theodaldus while also promising Dom Guido to eventually return to Pomposa, Brother Guido began to feel stuck in a state of limbo. He continued to oversee scribal copying and to teach, rehearse, and lead music for the Divine Office and Masses, but as time passed, he felt increasingly rootless. With the arrival of his fortieth birthday, and with his health still precarious as a result of his Roman sojourn, he even wondered how much longer he would live. Unsure of Michael's welfare and his own future, he prayed unceasingly for clarity.

Surely the sad event that ensued was not an answer to that prayer, although it did in fact serve to clarify Guido's path. On a warm Sunday in late spring, when Bishop Theodaldus was offering a service of blessing for the town's animals, a dog viciously bit him in the arm. The animal proved to be rabid, and within weeks Theodaldus fell dangerously ill with fever and convulsions.

As the bishop lay ailing in June, Guido brought the boys' choir to his bedside every day to serenade him with comforting hymns. Sometimes, writhing in pain, the bishop seemed not even to hear. But one day, after the boys had sung, he beckoned Guido to come closer.

"Thank you, Brother Guido," he said with difficulty, his once-booming voice reduced to a whisper. "That was beautiful. I thought I was already listening to the angels greeting me in heaven."

"Oh, please don't say such things," said Guido urgently. "We still need you here."

Theodaldus shook his head. "Thank you for all you have done for the Holy Church in Arezzo. It has been an honor to have you in my service."

"The honor has been mine to serve you, Lord Bishop," said Guido as tears welled in his eyes. "I can never adequately express my gratitude for all you have done for me. I was in hopeless misery and you were my rescue, my salvation."

"But I know you have been drawn to return to Pomposa since the abbot invited you back," said Theodaldus slowly. "And I know you have remained here out of loyalty to me. With my passing, there will be nothing to hold you back. You have my blessing to return to the abbey."

"I hope that day comes much later than you expect!"

exclaimed Guido, trying to offer at least some small measure of cheer.

But again the bishop shook his head, this time with a faraway look in his eyes. Realizing that the end was near, Guido sent for Dom Petro to administer the last rites. And less than an hour after this final blessing, with Guido kneeling by his bedside in prayer, Theodaldus closed his eyes for the last time.

Although they were almost the same age, Guido felt he had lost another father—the authority figure who had been his most active and energetic supporter. Heartbroken, he led the music for the solemn Requiem Mass in the Church of St. Donatus, the place of worship that the bishop himself had planned and brought to completion.

Months were bound to pass before word reached Rome and a new bishop was anointed. Guido sensed that the time was right to take advantage of this hiatus and return to Pomposa, especially in light of Theodaldus's deathbed blessing. As a fortuitous result of Guido's unfortunate illness, his assistant had gained ample experience in handling Arezzo's musical responsibilities. As a result, when Guido confided his plans, Canon Francesco felt sufficiently prepared to succeed his revered mentor.

Hoping to avoid any elaborate farewell, Guido nevertheless realized that with the death of Theodaldus, he needed to inform someone in the clergy of his intentions. Fortunately, he remembered that Dom Petro had been present when Dom Guido had invited him back to Pomposa.

"Dom Petro?" said Guido, approaching him after the next morning's Mass.

"Brother Guido, peace be with you. The singing of the choir was especially beautiful this morning."

"Thank you, and I'm sure they'll continue to sing beautifully after I'm gone."

"Don't talk like that," said Petro, misunderstanding Guido's meaning. "I know we feared we might lose you after we returned from Rome, but haven't you been in reasonable health of late?"

"I didn't mean after I've gone to my reward," said Guido with a smile. "But do you remember when the abbot of Pomposa invited me to go back to the abbey?"

"Of course."

"On his deathbed, Bishop Theodaldus gave me his blessing to return. I expect to leave within the week. Canon Francesco is fully prepared to succeed me here."

"This is quite sudden."

"I had stayed here only out of loyalty to the bishop. I was raised to be a monk, and as a monk I belong in a monastery. I've come to appreciate my life here, but frankly, it will be a relief to escape from all the priestly graft and simony."

Petro shrugged, all too well aware that Guido spoke the truth.

"I'll continue to do what I can to combat such behavior," said the canon apologetically.

"This may not fall under your jurisdiction," continued Guido, "but I'd like to ask Oliverio if he could accompany me on the journey."

"I will speak to him later today and make the necessary arrangements."

"Thank you," said Guido. "You and Canon Francesco are the two people here I will truly miss."

The ever-faithful Oliverio readily agreed to repeat his long-ago journey to Pomposa and back, this time to escort Guido in the opposite direction. Deciding they would leave in two days' time, the monk began gathering his possessions for the journey. Along with the few practical items he had brought with him from the abbey, he packed one copy of each of his books.

The morning of their departure, while Oliverio was loading the horses, Guido visited the music room, where Francesco was rehearsing with the boys' choir.

"I'm sorry to interrupt," said Guido as he entered.

"Not at all," said Francesco deferentially, gesturing for the monk to take the floor.

"My beloved choirboys," said Guido emotionally, "as you know, I'm called Brother Guido, not Father Guido. That's because I'm a monk, not a priest. And a monk's place is among his brother monks. I'm returning to my home abbey today, and it's far away. So I've come here to say goodbye."

"No!" screamed the boys, and a few burst into tears.

"Pay attention to Canon Francesco, and don't forget me," said Guido, fighting to keep from crying himself. He started to go, but Francesco had a sudden idea and stopped him.

"Boys, let's sing for Brother Guido one last time—the special chant he composed for us."

As Guido stood listening, tears running down his cheeks, the boys sang:

Ut queant laxis
Resonare fibris
Mira gestorum
Famuli tuorum,
Solve polluti
Labii reatum,
Sancte Johannes

Only then did Guido return to his chamber for one last sentimental task. Taking his father's four-decade-old chalice from the cupboard, he carefully wrapped it in a woolen kerchief and placed it in a leather satchel. Clutching his treasure tightly, he gave the room one last look and then turned to leave it forever.

Chapter Eighteen

THE RETURN TO POMPOSA

As the horses ambled their way north, both riders were content to proceed in silence. Guido in particular was all too well aware that, after years of being able to talk whenever he pleased, he was about to reenter an environment where speaking was severely limited. The journey was an ideal chance to reaccustom himself to keeping quiet.

Their intended route was the same as when Oliverio had traveled from Arezzo to Pomposa years earlier to fetch Guido. The first leg would take them to the Abbey of San Mercuriale, outside the walls of Forlì. The second day they were to proceed to Comacchio's monastery of Santa Maria in Auregiario, leaving only a half day's travel to reach Pomposa.

When Guido had visited San Mercuriale for the first time on his way to assume his post in Arezzo, he was an unknown monk who was delighted to receive the monastery's hospitality in anonymity. Arriving there this time, he was treated as a visiting celebrity. Of course Guido was aware that his writings and chant book were spreading across the Papal States, but he was unprepared for the fuss that was made on his behalf. At the end of a festive banquet in his honor, complete with generous slabs of beef, the monastery's choir even serenaded him with his own *Ut queant laxis*.

"I'm speechless," he responded. "And as anyone who knows me would agree, that's a rare phenomenon."

"We appreciate the opportunity to welcome such an important guest," said San Mercuriale's abbot.

"But I'm curious," said Guido. "How did you find out about *Ut queant laxis*? I only wrote about it in my *Ad invendiendum ignotum cantum*, and I sent the only complete copy of that treatise to a monk in Pomposa."

"Apparently that monk must have handed it off to the abbey's scriptorium to be copied. At any rate, a few months ago, Dom Guido sent us a copy with his compliments."

So my letter did reach Brother Michael, thought Guido. *And surely that means my letter to Dom Guido was delivered as well.* His spirits rose at the prospect that Michael's lot at Pomposa might have improved.

The next morning the monks of San Mercuriale lined up in procession to bid their celebrated guest farewell. Guido was greatly touched by their attentions and only hoped his reception back at Pomposa would be half as enthusiastic.

"You're quite a famous man, Brother Guido," said Oliverio as they continued north.

"By the grace of God," said Guido. "Earthly fame means nothing to me, but I'm gratified by the spread of my methods.

Especially since my ideas were so severely condemned when I first conceived them."

"I'm glad that you've lived long enough to see this," said Oliverio.

"Yet why have I been spared when our beloved patron's life was tragically cut short?" wondered Guido sadly, and they both crossed themselves in reverent memory of Bishop Theodaldus.

Around midday, the two stopped in a forest glade, tethered the horses to a tree, and sat on a fallen log to enjoy a simple meal. The singing of the birds and the rustling of the leaves lulled them into a relaxed reverie.

Suddenly they were startled by the sound of rapidly approaching horses. Within seconds they were surrounded by three riders bearing heavy wooden cudgels. Before Guido and Oliverio could begin to resist, the outlaws dismounted, tied the two travelers' arms behind their backs, and seized their two horses.

"Just keep quiet and nobody will get hurt," shouted the heaviest of the three, his beady eyes peering out from beneath an unruly thatch of red hair. Then, addressing his two accomplices, he growled, "Look through their baggage."

"Books," observed the shortest of the trio, a sullen codger with a gray beard. "We can barter these at a monastery library."

"What else?" barked the red-haired ringleader.

"Nothing much," said the bearded robber, rifling carelessly through Guido's few personal effects. But then he noticed the satchel. "Except—what's in here?" Pulling out the carefully wrapped object, he tore off the protective kerchief and gazed at the earthenware chalice. "Take a look at this," he said, tossing it high into the air in the redhead's general direction.

Guido's heart stopped as he stared upward, paralyzed in panic. For what seemed like an eternity, the cup appeared to hover in midair. As his terror-filled eyes followed the high arc of its perilous trajectory, he screamed, "No!"—certain that his long-treasured memento would drop and shatter into hundreds of pieces.

But by some miracle, the red-haired robber intercepted the chalice with one hand, bobbled it twice, and then caught it with both hands.

"Nice catch," said the third robber, silent up till now.

The redhead slowly turned the cup in his hands until the inscription was facing him. Long ago, this robber had actually learned to read.

"Guido?" he said, looking up at his two victims.

"Yes," responded Guido, his heart still pounding. "That's my name."

Still clutching the chalice, the robber approached the anxious monk and peered intently at his face. Despite the beard, something in Guido's visage seemed distantly familiar.

"Not the Guido who was an oblate at the abbey of Pomposa?"

The monk was thunderstruck. "Yes, the same Guido," he replied, now completely bewildered.

"It's me, Uberto!" exclaimed the redhead.

Guido remembered immediately. "Uberto! The boy who ran away!"

"And look at me now," sighed Uberto. "But at least it's better than being locked up in a damned monastery."

"I always wondered what had happened to you," said Guido quietly.

"Let's get going," snarled the gray-bearded robber abruptly.

"Here, you can keep this," said Uberto, carefully handing the chalice back to Guido. "And leave the books," he shouted to his cohorts, who grumbled as they replaced the volumes in the travelers' baggage.

"I'm sorry, but we have to take your horses," said Uberto awkwardly. "There's a monastery not too far away—San Vitale. Turn right at the next fork in the path and follow the road to Ravenna. You should be able to walk there before nightfall."

"Thank you," said Guido automatically, before realizing that he had scant cause to be thankful.

The other two robbers had remounted, each leading one of the stolen horses. Uberto quickly untied Guido and Oliverio, then climbed onto his own horse and galloped away with the others close behind.

"Lucky that he knew you," said Oliverio, relieved that at least neither of them had been harmed.

Guido nodded, bowed his head, and offered a silent prayer of thanks to the Blessed Virgin.

Uberto's directions were accurate; trudging on foot, the robbery victims approached the Benedictine monastery of San Vitale just before sunset. Identifying themselves and explaining their plight, they were quickly ushered into the cloister, where the heavy-jowled abbot made an even bigger fuss than had the abbot at San Mercuriale.

"*The* Guido of Arezzo?" he exclaimed. "What an honor to receive you!"

"Thank you, and bless you for your welcome," said Guido. "I apologize for this unexpected intrusion."

"No, not at all," said the abbot. "The privilege is entirely ours. Our cantor has been using your methods faithfully ever since an emissary from Pope John brought us a copy of your chant book and prologue."

This was the first Guido had heard of the late pope's efforts on his behalf. With a start, he realized that his fame must be even more widespread than he had suspected.

The monk and his companion were treated to another celebratory banquet, this one featuring roast duck, and then were quartered in the best room of the guesthouse. The abbot insisted on giving them two horses, though Oliverio promised to return one of them on his journey home. The next morning the monks serenaded Guido with hymns they had learned from his chant book and then sent the visitors on their way with prayers for safe travels. Because of the unexpected detour, Guido and Oliverio now headed directly for Pomposa, with no need to stop in Comacchio.

As the two travelers drew ever closer to their destination, Guido's mind was again flooded with memories. Time had not softened the pain of his persecution. But he also recalled his special companionship with Brother Michael. His heart welled with joyful anticipation as he imagined a return to the life to which God had called him and a long-awaited reunion with his long-suffering friend.

At last the familiar bell tower appeared on the horizon, and soon Guido and Oliverio reached the abbey. Because Guido's decision to return had been so sudden, he had not even gone to the trouble of sending word of his impending arrival, since any messenger would have taken almost as long to make the journey. So for the abbey, his appearance was a complete but entirely pleasant surprise. Dom Guido was quickly summoned to meet Brother Guido in the cloister.

"The prodigal son returns!" the abbot exclaimed, spotting Guido across the courtyard.

"Thank you, Lord Abbot," said Guido, bowing reverently—although he couldn't help thinking that in this case the spiritual father had been more prodigal than the son. "It's good to be home."

"Someone go ring the bell," directed the abbot. "We must all gather to welcome our returning brother."

As the tolling reverberated from the bell tower, the monks—many of them unfamiliar to Guido—swarmed into the cloister, puzzled by the unexpected summons. Guido surveyed their faces with increasing disappointment: There was no sign of Michael.

"Brothers, if you don't remember Brother Guido from his earlier years here"—the abbot then cleared his throat in embarrassment at having approached a touchy subject—"you know him from his chant book and his music treatises, which we use here every day. Please welcome him back with the sign of peace."

Lining up behind the now-ancient Prior Pangratio according to their current hierarchy, one by one the monks greeted Guido and clasped his hand, then dispersed to resume their usual duties.

Turning to the abbot, Guido began, "I didn't see—"

"I'm afraid your uncle, Brother Cristofano, breathed his last shortly after Easter," said Dom Guido, misunderstanding the monk's intent.

At least I was able to honor his wishes by conveying his greetings to our family, reflected Guido. But before he could resume his original thought and ask about Brother Michael, he belatedly noticed that his escort had been standing patiently all this time in the covered walkway.

"I'm sorry—this is Oliverio," said Guido. "He kindly accompanied me here. I hope he can be accommodated in the guest quarters for the night."

"Certainly," said the abbot, dispatching a senior monk to make the necessary arrangements. "And I will find special quarters for you as well. As our new cantor, there's no need for you to sleep on the dormitory floor."

"I'm greatly obliged," said Guido. "I'm afraid I've gotten spoiled sleeping on a feather mattress during all my years in Arezzo."

"Follow me to my chambers—I'm sure we have much to discuss."

"Of course," said Guido, though now he was determined to ask the question that had been on his lips since he moment he arrived. With rising trepidation, he continued, "But first, may I ask where I could find my friend Brother Michael?"

"Oh, I thought you might have heard."

Guido instantly feared the worst, but the abbot continued, "Brother Michael has his own cell adjoining the infirmary."

Relieved yet also newly alarmed, Guido asked, "Why the infirmary? What happened?"

"After you left us," Dom Guido began hesitantly, "Brother Anselmo was . . . he was not entirely able to forgive Brother Michael for his part in furthering your methods. As a disciplinary measure to maintain peace within the community, Michael was dismissed from the choir and was assigned the humble role of the abbey's chamberlain." The abbot paused.

Anxious to know the rest of the story, Guido said, "Yes, please go on."

"As chamberlain," resumed the abbot, "Brother Michael was responsible for keeping the exterior of the buildings in good repair, and he performed his duties faithfully. Upon receiving your letter," the abbot cleared his throat, "I relieved him of that duty, but he had almost finished repairing the tiles over the church portico, and he insisted on completing the job. The very next day, after he had climbed to a dangerous height on the roof, a tool slipped out of his hand, and when he tried to grab it, he lost his balance and slid over the edge. By the grace of God, a hedge broke his fall, but I'm afraid he was badly injured."

Guido gasped.

"He broke both of his legs. His health has gradually recovered, but he can no longer walk."

"May I see him now, please?" asked Guido urgently.

"Of course," said the abbot, changing direction to

head toward the infirmary. On arriving there, he gestured silently toward Michael's cell and took his leave.

Guido tiptoed slowly toward the open door. He could see Michael seated on a bench, reading a book, with his back braced against the wall, his legs dangling uselessly toward the floor. Approaching more closely, Guido sadly noticed what a toll Michael's years of suffering had taken. His once-angelic looks were now hardened and wrinkled, and his formerly alabaster skin was rough and brown from working in the sun.

But his smile was as beatific as ever, as Guido immediately discovered when he called Michael's name.

"Guido! Am I dreaming or are you really here?" asked Michael, immediately recognizing his friend despite the intervening years.

"I'm really here," Guido assured him, approaching more closely. "And here to stay. I'm the new cantor."

"What wonderful news! I wish I could stand and give you a proper greeting."

"Don't worry, Dom Guido told me about your accident. I'm so sorry."

"You mean you never received my last letter, telling you what happened?"

"No—in fact, I never even knew whether you had received *my* letter until I found out that you'd had it copied."

"All but the page with *Ubi caritas*," said Michael with a sudden surge of emotion.

Guido clasped both of Michael's hands and held them tightly.

"I see you've grown a beard," said Michael finally.

"Yes, to hide my bony face."

"There's nothing wrong with your face," Michael responded softly.

Guido smiled wearily. "I can see the years of suffering in yours."

"At least since my accident I'm excused from all manual labor—and even from singing," said Michael with a smile. "I can spend all my days reading and studying. A servant brings me my meals and books from the library."

"That servant can be reassigned," said Guido gently. "I'm your servant now."

"But didn't you say you're the new cantor?"

"Yes," replied Guido, "but when I am not attending to my music, I will be at your faithful service."

Chapter Nineteen

A NEW CALL

When Guido went back to speak with the abbot, Dom Guido led him to the ground floor of the dormitory, where his books and other possessions had been placed in a small private cell. There was barely enough room for a mattress and a tiny wooden table. But after years of living in his own room at Arezzo, Guido was relieved to be assigned private quarters, however cramped. Quickly finding his leather satchel, he carefully removed the "Guido" chalice, unwrapped it, and placed it safely on the table.

"I had one of the feather mattresses brought here from the guest quarters," said the abbot, pleased to see that the chalice had survived all these years. "If Bishop Cunibert ever comes back for another inspection, I can say you have a bad back."

"Thank you, Lord Abbot," said Guido, who could have done without the reminder of Cunibert's last visit.

"I've reserved a special corner of the scriptorium for you, with your own supply of parchment, and all the monks who labor there are at your disposal to make copies of your writings."

Guido nodded in gratitude.

"Brother Simoneto has been especially enthusiastic about adopting your methods. He has been acting as cantor since Brother Anselmo's passing, but has been fully prepared to hand over the reins whenever you might arrive."

"I look forward to speaking with him about how to begin my duties with the least disruption of his routines," said Guido, recalling Simoneto's early enthusiasm for his methods.

"Is there anything else I can do to welcome you back?" asked the abbot, clearly trying his best to atone for having once made the monk's life so miserable.

"There is," answered Guido firmly. "When Brother Michael was a novice, I was entrusted with the guardianship of his soul. His soul may no longer need a guardian, but the same cannot be said of his broken body. I would like to be responsible for his care."

"But won't you be busy enough with your musical responsibilities?" asked the abbot.

"I'm sure Brother Simoneto can assist me."

"Very well," said the abbot, guiltily acquiescing to reverse the last of his previous punishments. "As St. Benedict has said, 'Before and above all things, care must be taken of the sick, that they be served in very truth as Christ is served; because He hath said, 'As long as you did it to one of these, my least brethren, you did it to Me.'"

Early the next morning, under gray skies, Guido bade an emotional farewell to the loyal Oliverio.

"Thank you for all your kindnesses," said the monk. "Godspeed on your return to Arezzo."

"It has always been a pleasure to serve you," responded Oliverio.

"I will never forget dear Luca," said Guido softly.

"God bless you," said the servant with a bow before mounting his horse and taking his leave.

Guido kept watching the path until his last connection to Arezzo had disappeared.

At his first music rehearsal later that morning, Guido quickly discovered how conscientiously Simoneto had been following his methods, and so the cantorial transition was surprisingly smooth. Leading the singing for the Divine Office and Masses was especially rewarding back in the resonant acoustics of the candlelit Church of St. Maria. And Guido's years of training the boys' choir in Arezzo made him a natural teacher for the monastery's latest oblates. Learning the chants from notated music rather than by rote, the boys little realized that they were being spared years of frustrating trial and error.

Other than recopying books that had fallen apart from overuse, the scribes in the scriptorium now devoted their efforts almost exclusively to spreading the works of the abbey's most famous monk. Guido found renewed pleasure in supervising their copying of his chant book and treatises. Occasionally, when revisiting the old texts, he was even inspired to dictate new interpolations.

But Guido's moments of greatest contentment were spent by the side of Brother Michael. Often they sat in silence, simply reading or meditating. But as his friend's official guardian, Guido felt no compunction about ignoring the usual Benedictine vow of silence—especially after his years at Arezzo had accustomed him to speaking his mind at will. And in any case, the two monks' conversations aroused scant notice, since visits to Brother Michael by the abbot and prior were exceedingly rare.

"They can't bear to look at you," observed Guido one afternoon. "You're a living reminder of what a terrible mistake they made."

"It's just as well," said Michael. "At this point I prefer solitude."

"Yet my guilt was as great as theirs. Your punishment was all because of me."

"You forget that I'm the one who asked you to do what we were punished for," said Michael reassuringly.

"But when I think of you slipping off that roof—" said Guido, shaking his head, too upset to finish the thought.

"I did think I would die," recalled Michael calmly. "I'm still amazed to be alive."

"I'm sure the angels were disappointed."

"No, they're glad I'm not up there trying to sing."

"Don't be silly," said Guido. "In heaven, everyone sings perfectly."

"Maybe so, but I wonder: Do the angels and the saints in heaven sing the same chants that we sing on earth?"

Guido thought for a moment before responding. "I believe

that heaven has its own music, more beautiful than anything we mortals could ever imagine."

"But surely they at least sing *Ut queant laxis*," said Michael with a smile. "Or if they don't, they will when you get there."

With Guido's return to Pomposa, it became increasingly common for travelers to make pilgrimages to the monastery in hopes of meeting the famous monk and learning about his musical ideas firsthand. He always welcomed them cordially, and those who had come from cathedrals or other abbeys were typically sent home with a copy of his chant book, if one could be spared. Thus Guido's fame continued to spread across the Italian peninsula and even to regions further north.

One day, an entire delegation arrived from a greater distance than any previous visitors. The half-dozen monks had traveled all the way from St. Pierre des Fossés, located southeast of Paris. A papal emissary visiting that abbey had told them about the celebrated musician whose methods had revolutionized the teaching of chant singing, and they had come to gain direct knowledge of his innovations. The abbot welcomed them warmly and gave Guido a sabbatical from his daily cantorial duties—with Brother Simoneto ably substituting—so that he could devote as much time as possible to educating the French visitors.

Beginning with *Micrologus* and continuing with the *Prologus* and *Regule*, Guido read his treatises aloud, answered questions, and illustrated his points with examples from his chant book. Then he continued with *Ad invendiendum ignotum cantum,* teaching his new disciples the increasingly popular *Ut queant laxis.* Finally, he showed them a diagram of his left palm and drilled them in the scale patterns of the Guidonian Hand.

After three weeks, the French monks were well trained and ready to begin the long journey back to their abbey. As a farewell gesture, Dom Guido mounted a lavish celebratory banquet, complete with roast pheasant. But Guido refused to attend unless Brother Michael could be carried to the refectory to enjoy the occasion with the rest of the brotherhood. The abbot warily agreed, and so—carried by four of the abbey's sturdiest monks— Michael was placed in a seat of honor next to Guido, the abbot, and the six visitors.

At the conclusion of the meal, Michael's burly escorts again lifted him to their shoulders, returning him safely to his cell. Guido followed close behind, and for many long minutes he and Michael sat quietly, basking in the triumphant occasion.

"I never realized before just how famous you are," said Michael finally.

"To God be the glory," responded Guido.

"Yes, but as we know from the parable of the talents, not all who receive divine gifts put those gifts to good use. It's you and you alone who produced these great achievements. And whether or not you care about earthly fame, you richly deserve every tribute you receive."

"But Michael," said Guido quietly, "it was all because of you."

"What are you talking about?" said Michael skeptically.

"Everything I devised—notating music on a staff, improving how singers are taught—it all started just because I wanted to help you."

Michael smiled, his eyes twinkling. "I guess it's lucky I was such a slow learner."

Guido's health had never fully recovered from the Roman vapors. Fortunately, as cantor, he was excused from the usual requirement of manual labor, so when the other monks were busy with their daily tasks, he was able to attend to Michael. Because Guido tired easily, he received a special dispensation to delegate the Matins service to Brother Simoneto so that he could get additional sleep. Of course there were many aspects of the monastery's operations that the always-opinionated monk felt could be done more effectively, and he was never shy about sharing his views at chapter meetings, usually in vain. But altogether he led a satisfying life, and as the months and years passed, Guido had no doubt whatsoever that he would spend the remainder of his days at Pomposa.

When a slim young monk in a white cassock appeared at the monastery's entrance one day and asked to see Brother Guido, those who welcomed him assumed that he was just another of the many pilgrims seeking to meet the widely known musician and perhaps to learn more about his methods. Guido made the same assumption when he was summoned to meet the traveler in the cloister.

"Good afternoon, brother, and welcome. I am Brother Guido, cantor of Pomposa Abbey."

"Thank you for receiving me," said the visitor in a high, reedy voice. "I am Brother Zilio from the Camaldolese monastery of Santa Croce di Fonte Avellana."

"Camaldolese? That would explain your white cassock," responded Guido. "And where exactly is Santa Croce?"

"In Serra Sant'Abbondio, near Avellana in the Marche region, not far from here to the east."

"I believe I've heard of it," said Guido. "If you'd like to come to the library, I can show you my chant book and treatises. And if you're able to stay the night in our guest quarters, perhaps you'd like to watch me rehearse music with the other monks tomorrow morning."

"All of that sounds most pleasant and I appreciate your generous offers," responded Zilio. "But I'm afraid you misunderstand the reason for my visit."

"Oh?" said Guido, suddenly apprehensive. "Have you come to lodge some kind of complaint against me?"

"Oh, no, nothing like that," laughed Zilio. "I've actually come to deliver a message from our abbot, Dom Rambaldo."

"I see. And the message?"

"Our Lord Abbot would like to invite you to join Santa Croce di Fonte Avellana as our new prior."

"What?" said Guido, unsure that he had heard correctly. But he heard exactly the same words when Zilio repeated them.

"Dom Rambaldo is keenly interested in elevating the quality of the music we offer to God's glory," said Zilio, "and surely no one else could be more qualified to lead that effort."

"But that would seem to be the responsibility of your cantor," said Guido, still puzzled. "You're asking me to help manage the day-to-day affairs of the whole monastery."

"With special attention to supervising our cantor, but yes, you would be the abbot's second-in-command."

"Whatever gave Dom Rambaldo the idea of asking me?"

"He had heard that at Pomposa you hold strong opinions about how things ought to be done. He tends to be—shall we say, less decisive. So he would welcome a prior who has firm convictions like yours."

"I can't imagine how such rumors could have gotten started," said Guido, raising his eyebrows with a wry smile.

"He has asked me to stay here until you give me your answer," continued Zilio. "And if your answer is yes, to escort you back to Santa Croce."

"But I'm old and not in the best of health. Who knows how many years of service I have left to give to Dom Rambaldo?"

"That is in God's hands."

So far, Guido had found the proposal completely out of the question. But the more the two discussed it, the more intrigued he became.

"Let me ask you this," he said after further exchanges. "I hold a special responsibility here to care for an injured monk who can no longer walk. If he could be transported there, would he be allowed to join your brotherhood as well?"

"Of course," said Zilio. "Are we not commanded to care for the lame and the halt? And our infirmary is a special preoccupation of the abbot. Perhaps your crippled monk would receive even better care with us."

By now this possible leap into the unknown had genuinely piqued Guido's curiosity. "Could you explain to me the difference between Camaldolese and Benedictine monasteries?" he asked. "I was trained according to the Rule of St. Benedict, so I have no experience with your tradition."

"Our order was founded by St. Romuald of Ravenna, who was a Benedictine monk himself," answered Zilio. "It came to be called Camaldolese after he founded the hermitage and monastery of Camaldoli, in the mountains of Tuscany, with the permission of Bishop Theodaldus of Arezzo."

"My dearly departed superior!" exclaimed Guido. "May he rest in peace."

"Amen." After a moment of silence, Zilio continued, "St. Romuald also founded our abbey near Avellana. Above all, he sought to combine the solitary life of the hermit with the traditional monastic life of the cloister."

"But exactly how does that work in actual practice?"

"Our monks live in solitary cells but still participate in the monastery's communal life, worshipping together in the church and sharing meals in the refectory. As the monks grow older, they find greater spiritual peace in the isolation of the hermitage and become less involved with their fellow monks in the monastery."

"And yet you think an old monk like me should be helping manage the monastery's affairs instead of creeping toward solitude?" asked Guido teasingly. "At any rate, please, stay the night with us. This matter will require a great deal of thought. And of course I would need to discuss the question with my abbot and my musical assistant . . . and others," he added, already thinking of Michael.

"As I told you," responded Zilio, "my abbot has given me leave to remain here until I can return with your answer—and, I hope, with you."

Guido knew that he could not even consider the offer without conferring with Dom Guido and Brother Simoneto. But the first person he consulted was Michael.

"It's a wonderful opportunity," said Michael enthusiastically. "And as prior you'd have a say in running things, which I'm sure would suit you well."

"Apparently word of my outspoken opinions has leaked out of our chapter meetings," said Guido with a shrug.

"Best of all, you can spread your musical methods to an entirely new religious community. Brother Simoneto will carry on your tradition here, while you go on to teach another monastery the gospel according to Guido."

Ignoring that bit of overstatement, Guido continued, "It's true that leading the music here is no longer much of a challenge."

"You've succeeded all too well."

"Since this is the gift God has given me, perhaps He wants me to use it in new ways," said Guido pensively. "But if Abbot Guido permits me to go, I will request that you go to Santa Croce di Fonte Avellana as well."

"Would they even accept me there—a useless cripple?" asked Michael skeptically.

"Don't talk like that. And yes, I've already confirmed that you would be welcome."

"But how would I get there?"

"I can arrange for horses or oxen to pull a cart you could ride in. The distance isn't that great."

Inwardly, Michael was frightened by the thought of an arduous journey and a whole new living situation. But he was loath to hold his friend back.

"You shouldn't let this chance pass by," said Michael. "Don't worry about me. You go ahead, and I'll try to get stronger and follow you later."

After several days of meditation and prayer, Guido met with Dom Guido and Brother Simoneto, still not having made up his mind. Although greatly surprised, both warmly congratulated Guido on the news. Simoneto promised to maintain the cantor's musical legacy, and this satisfied the abbot sufficiently to give the move his reluctant blessing. For a second and no doubt final time, the spiritual father would be bidding farewell to his monastic son. And so at last Guido summoned Brother Zilio and agreed to go to Santa Croce.

Because Zilio was tasked with escorting the prior-designate to his new post as soon as possible, Guido was obliged to immediately begin packing his books and his few personal effects for yet another momentous journey. As always, the last and most important possession to be safely stowed was his father's ceramic chalice, where the name "Guido" was still clearly visible.

The next morning, before meeting Zilio by the bell tower, Guido paid one last visit to his dearest friend.

"Goodbye for now, Michael," said Guido, firmly clasping the seated monk's hands. "Send word when you feel strong enough to join me."

"Of course," Michael assured him. "Godspeed on your journey!" But a vise seemed to tighten around his heart, and he could not escape the painful thought that he would never see Guido again.

Inwardly seized by the same fear, Guido impulsively bent toward his seated friend and squeezed him tightly. Michael held Guido just as closely; neither wanted to let go. At last Guido pulled back so that he and Michael were face to face, their foreheads only inches apart. Solemnly, he gave Michael the kiss of peace and then stood and hurried toward the cloister before he could change his mind.

As he and Zilio rode on horseback toward Serra Sant'Abbondio, Guido turned back to gaze at Pomposa's majestic bell tower. In his heart he knew he was seeing it for the last time.

Chapter Twenty

THE END OF THE JOURNEY

Before the day ended, Guido's eyes beheld an equally impressive site: the monumental complex of white stone buildings that housed Santa Croce di Fonte Avellana. Nestled in green forested hills, the abbey was crowned by a tall, square bell tower and centered around a small church with an arching roof and a row of high, clear windows.

Brother Zilio escorted Guido directly to the chapter house, where he presented the new arrival to Abbot Rambaldo, a slight, middle-aged worthy with a tonsured ring of sandy brown hair. The abbot began by giving Guido a Camaldolese white cassock to replace his Benedictine black one.

"I'm delighted to welcome you to our brotherhood," said Rambaldo cheerily.

"I'm honored by your faith in my abilities," responded Guido. "And I hope you'll still be delighted once you discover how opinionated I can be."

"I'm delighted already," said the abbot. "I find that I always see both sides of every question, to the point where I can never make up my mind about anything. And then nothing gets decided, and matters continue to drift along—"

"I think we're going to work together very well," said Guido with a smile.

The abbot led Guido to his new cell, a tiny but sunny room on an upper floor with a window overlooking the gardens. High in one corner was a triangular shelf. *The perfect spot for my father's chalice*, thought Guido, carefully unpacking the earthenware cup and standing on tiptoe to set it in its new place of honor.

Rambaldo then introduced him to Brother Matheo, the monastery's young and energetic cantor, who was excited to meet the celebrated Guido and eager to enlist his expertise in raising the choir's musical standards. Guido shared copies of his treatises and chant book and was delighted when the monks quickly learned *Ut queant laxis* and began applying its pattern to learning new chants.

Within a few short weeks, the new prior had settled comfortably into his responsibilities—supervising Matheo's singing rehearsals, overseeing the scribes who were making copies of his works, and collaborating closely with the abbot to keep the monastery running smoothly. *If only Brother Michael would arrive*, thought Guido, *my happiness here would be complete.*

Not all was smooth sailing. At a chapter meeting soon after Guido's arrival, a long-simmering dispute bubbled over.

"It's all well and good to allow monks to leave our monastery dwellings to live in greater solitude in our hermitage," said a thin young monk. "But many are doing this just to avoid manual labor."

"I'm no longer capable of manual labor," retorted a stooped older monk.

"I'm not talking about you," said the first monk.

"And exactly who are you talking about?" asked a heavyset denizen of the hermitage.

Ignoring that last comment, the young monk continued, "The fact is that much of our work now goes undone, because not enough of us are left in the monastery to do it all. So we must hire more servants to do it, which leaves us with fewer resources to distribute to the poor and needy."

"Would you work me to the bone till I collapse and die?" asked the heavyset monk angrily. "Do you imagine I could still labor on earth after my spirit has left my body?"

"Brothers, brothers!" called the abbot in a conciliatory tone. "There's no need to prolong this argument any further. The only question is . . . ." His voice trailed off, for he had long pondered the issue without ever arriving at a satisfactory answer. Helplessly, he looked at Guido.

"Even if a monk can no longer do manual labor, he can still contribute to the work of the community by copying manuscripts in the scriptorium," said Guido firmly.

A murmur of surprise rippled through the assembly.

"And if his hand trembles too much for him to work in the scriptorium, he can carry a pail and sprinkle water on the flowers in the garden," Guido continued. "Unless a monk is confined to the infirmary, he should contribute to the life of our abbey, whether he dwells in solitary meditation in the hermitage or among his brothers in the cloister."

Abbot Rambaldo stared at Guido in wonder. But the new prior wasn't finished.

"To better organize our procedures," said Guido, "I ask that, henceforth, all who seek to leave the cloister to enter the hermitage must receive my approval to do so."

The pronouncement was met with an uneasy silence.

"Your *prior* approval?" asked a waggish monk from the rear of the room, finally breaking the tension.

"Thank you, Prior Guido," said the abbot as the laughter in the room subsided, relieved that his new lieutenant had jumped so readily into the fray. "You will all be expected to observe the prior's new policies."

Needless to say, Guido's pronouncements did not please everyone, but most monks were relieved to be spared the abbot's constant, if well-intentioned, dithering. And the prior himself was unfazed by the brothers' occasional grumbling, as long as he was the one who got to make the decisions.

Part of his mind, however, was always focused back toward Pomposa, hoping that Brother Michael was gaining sufficient strength to make the journey to Santa Croce. Any time a visitor arrived from the west, Guido peppered him with questions, convinced that surely Michael would have sent word of his imminent arrival. But no one who had passed through Pomposa brought any news of his friend.

In fact, most such visitors had first journeyed to Pomposa to learn from the famous Guido and had come to Santa Croce only after being redirected to his new monastery. He always patiently tutored the musical pilgrims in his methods and sent them on their way to spread his teachings even more widely.

Finally, one day as Guido was quietly reading a psalm aloud in his cell, an oblate came timidly to his door.

"A monk from Pomposa is here to see you," said the boy.

"Is he a monk who has lost the use of his legs?" asked Guido, suddenly animated.

"No, Prior Guido. This monk can walk just like you or I."

"Then he's here to tell me that Brother Michael is on his way and that we need to prepare a cell for him near the infirmary," exclaimed Guido, already hurrying toward the cloister.

"He didn't say, Lord Prior," said the boy, running to keep up. "He only said he needed to deliver a message to you personally."

Guido rushed even more quickly until the oblate caught up and led him toward the visitor. To his surprise, waiting in the cloister was his successor as Pomposa's cantor.

"This is unexpected, Brother Simoneto," said Guido, panting from his exertions.

"Lord Prior," said Simoneto gravely, "I thought I should come myself."

"When will Brother Michael be arriving?" asked Guido eagerly. "Have you come to make the necessary arrangements?"

Simoneto paused, then clasped the prior's hands. "I'm heartbroken to tell you that Brother Michael has gone to his reward."

"No!" exclaimed Guido, collapsing as if he had been stabbed in the heart.

"After you left, he grew steadily weaker, and eventually he

was no longer taking any nourishment. Blessedly, he was in no pain, and at the end he was at peace."

"I am to blame for this. If I hadn't left Pomposa, he would still be alive. My ambition has cost my dearest friend his life."

Brother Simoneto could barely hold back the tears. "I know in the very depths of my soul that Michael wouldn't have wanted you to feel that way," he said gently. "I know that your welfare was more important to him than life itself."

Guido merely shook his head, moaning piteously.

"I can even tell you how I know that," said Simoneto. "After we had administered the last rites, just before he expired, he asked me to give you this. He . . . he had been pressing it to his heart." Guido immediately recognized the second page of his long-ago letter, where he had written out the music of *Ubi caritas*.

"And he made me promise to sing it to you," continued Simoneto. His voice quavering with emotion, the cantor sang the same words that Guido had conveyed musically to his friend:

> *Where charity and love are, God is there.*
> *Love of Christ has gathered us into one.*

Guido returned to his cell. Sunlight was still streaming through the casement window, but all sunlight had faded from the monk's existence. Tightly clutching the *Ubi caritas* page, he collapsed on his mattress, knowing in his heart that he would never be able to resume his monastic duties.

Over the coming days, a stream of visitors appeared to

pay their last respects. Abbot Rambaldo, Brother Matheo, and Brother Zilio came daily to offer encouragement and comfort. Alerted by Brother Simoneto, even Dom Guido made the journey from Pomposa to say farewell. Prior Guido remained fully conscious and responsive, but he was inconsolable. His only aspiration was to follow Brother Michael into the heavenly hereafter.

In the moments when he was left alone, Guido gazed across his cell at the "Guido" chalice resting on the tiny corner shelf. Once, when a servant came to take away the meal he had barely touched, the bedridden prior asked him to move the little cup closer to the shelf's edge so that he could see it more clearly.

Staring at the earthenware chalice, knowing that it was exactly as old as he was, Guido thought back on his eventful life. Who would've guessed that a poor potter's son who grew up humming along with his father's pottery wheel would end up giving singing lessons to a pope? He thought of his family, who first brought him to hear the choir at the cathedral in Arezzo, and especially his mother, who had set him on the path of a religious life; of his mentor-turned-antagonist, Brother Anselmo, and the turmoil that had forced him to leave Pomposa; of Uberto, the boy who had fled Pomposa so many years earlier, now a marauding thief; of his beloved patron at Arezzo, Bishop Theodaldus, and the books he inspired Guido to write; of Pope John XIX, the corrupt prelate who had helped spread Guido's fame across Italy and beyond.

Most of all, he thought of Brother Michael and of the communion of souls they had shared from the day of their earliest meeting. At first Guido was still consumed with guilt, believing that he had hastened his friend's death. But deep inside he knew that Michael would have insisted he was not to blame. With his sweet, generous spirit, Michael always saw the best in everyone. Knowing they would soon be reunited among the heavenly hosts, Guido finally allowed himself to feel at peace.

Lying prostrate on the mattress, the prior slowly raised his left hand to his face. Peering at the palm and visualizing the Guidonian Hand, he could imagine each note of the scale across the fingertips and joints. In his head, he heard the tones rising and merging into an angelic strain sung by Michael in paradise: *Ubi caritas*. Slipping a hand beneath his scapular, he pressed the treasured manuscript against his heart.

After Guido had failed to eat anything for two days, Abbot Rambaldo heard his final confession and offered him Holy Viaticum as sustenance for his final journey. Brother Matheo brought Santa Croce's entire monastic choir to stand beneath the prior's window and serenade him. They sang many of Guido's favorite hymns and then closed with his own *Ut queant laxis*. For the first time since his collapse, a faint smile spread across the dying prior's wrinkled face. The singers performed his chant perfectly, and Guido could rest assured that the same practical melody was being sung in abbeys and churches throughout the land.

With the last sweet sounds of the chant fading in the afternoon air, Guido gave a convulsive cough that rattled everything in his tiny cell. The vibration set the little chalice teetering at the edge of the shelf, and after bouncing on the wooden ledge, it fell and crashed on the stone floor below. As Guido breathed his last breath, the chalice shattered into hundreds of pieces, its shards scattering in all directions—just as the monk's revolutionary ideas had spread throughout his lifetime and would continue to spread even farther for centuries to come.

Afterword

The few known facts of Guido of Arezzo's life, as outlined in the preface, were the starting point for this biographical tale. As further elaboration, I have also credited Guido with innovations associated with him but for which he might or might not have been personally responsible—composing the melody of *Ut queant laxis* and devising the Guidonian Hand. Extrapolating from these details and from accounts of medieval religious life, I have developed a fuller narrative that—albeit largely fictitious—is, I hope, historically plausible.

Although many of the book's characters are invented, others are based on actual historical personages. In addition to Guido himself, these include Brother Michael, his friend and fellow monk; Dom Guido, the abbot of the monastery at Pomposa; Bishop Theodaldus of Arezzo; Dom Petro, prefect of the canons at Arezzo; an abbot, Dom Grimaldus; Archbishop Eriberto of Ravenna; the architect Adabertus Maginardo; and Popes Benedict VIII and John XIX.

The novel's chronology follows the few dates that are known with some degree of certainty: the tenure of Dom Guido as abbot of Pomposa (998–1046), the design (1026) and dedication

(November 12, 1032) of Maginardo's Church of St. Donatus at Arezzo, the death of Pope John XIX (around October 1032), and the death of Bishop Theodaldus (June 12, 1036). Scholarly estimates of the date of Guido's birth range from 991 to 998, and he supposedly declared that he was thirty-four years old when he completed his *Micrologus*. But to cite any of these specific years would invite the reader to wonder about the dates of many more significant events in Guido's life for which no chronological information is available. It seemed more prudent to let the story flow from one incident to the next without trying to pin down specifics on a largely fictitious calendar. Thus, other than the millennium of AD 1000, no exact years are mentioned.

Summaries of and quotations from Guido's surviving treatises are factual, although the quotations are translated from the original Latin more freely than in scholarly sources. I took still greater liberties only in the opening section of the *Epistola* to Michael; my version of that text is heavily abridged, and the "lost" page and last two sentences are entirely my inventions.

I also offer a new interpretation of one of the *Epistola*'s more confusing passages. After recounting his brief Roman sojourn, Guido wrote that "a few days later" he met with Dom Guido, the abbot of Pomposa. Some have assumed that they met in Rome, but Guido had already said that he couldn't remain there long, and it would have been quite a coincidence if both Guido and the abbot from faraway Pomposa happened to be in Rome at the same time. Others assume that the two met in Pomposa; but it was during this meeting that the abbot asked Guido to come to Pomposa, which he could scarcely have done if they were already there. And Guido went on to tell Michael, who clearly *was* in Pomposa, that he could not come to him yet. I hypothesize that Guido returned from Rome to Arezzo and that the meeting took place there, the abbot having come to Arezzo for the express purpose of trying to lure Guido back to Pomposa.

All abbeys and monasteries mentioned in the novel actually existed in the first half of the eleventh century. The book's details about medieval monastic life are largely based on secondary sources that, in turn, are based on the records of those monasteries that documented their practices most extensively, notably Cluny in France. The medieval abbey at Pomposa apparently left no comparable documentation. Although the point of St. Benedict's Rule was to standardize practices among the Catholic Church's far-flung monasteries, it seems plausible that there was some degree of variation in monastic practices, and so I have allowed myself a degree of latitude in depicting life at Pomposa.

I have taken two additional, more specific liberties. The Fourth Lateran Council of 1215 mandated that bishops were to make visitations to inspect the monasteries in their jurisdictions. Speculating that this decree could have served to codify an already existing practice, I have incorporated such a visitation into this story. And although construction of Pomposa Abbey's bell tower was not begun until 1063, well after Guido's death (generally dated around 1050), I could not resist including that historic monastery's most distinctive architectural feature.

In passages relating to music theory, I have done my best to steer clear of the scholarly controversy over whether Guido's theoretical system was based on the hexachord (six-note scale), as seemingly implied by the six-note scale of *Ut queant laxis*, or—as Stefano Mengozzi argues in his book *The Renaissance Reform of Medieval Music Theory: Guido of Arezzo between Myth and History*—on the seven-note scale as repeated at the octave. I have also sidestepped Guido's own shifting opinions as to whether the note B could be altered to B-flat to avoid the tritone between F and B, an adjustment sanctioned in *Micrologus* but disallowed in the *Epistola*. And I have intentionally skirted the inconvenient fact that—although the solmization syllables *ut (do)-re-mi-fa-sol-la-ti* are now universally equated with, respectively, the tonic through leading-tone degrees of the scale—in the chant *Ut queant laxis*, the tonal center is actually *re*, not *ut*.

Key sources are gratefully acknowledged. An English translation of *Micrologus* appears in *Hucbald, Guido, and John on Music: Three Medieval Treatises*, translated by Warren Babb and edited with introductions by Claude V. Palisca (Yale University Press, 1978). Guido's other three treatises are translated in *Guido d'Arezzo's* Regule rithmice, Prologus in antiphonarium, *and* Epistola ad Michahelem: *A Critical Text and Translation* by Dolores Pesce (The Institute of Mediaeval Music, 1999). Book chapters and journal articles on medieval music education by Susan Boynton of Columbia University are particularly valuable sources on that subject.

The Guido who emerges from his writings is a man who knows he's right and isn't afraid to say so. Whatever my inventions and liberties, I hope that the same character emerges from the pages of this novel.

About the Author

Kingsley Day has written and composed numerous works for the stage, including (with Philip LaZebnik) the musical *Summer Stock Murder* and the comedy *Tour de Farce*, both produced multiple times in the US and abroad. His critically acclaimed score for Gilbert & Sullivan's *Thespis*, for which Sullivan's original score is lost, has received four Chicago-area productions. For Chicago's City Lit Theater, he has composed incidental music for *Prometheus Bound*, *The Tempest*, *London Assurance*, and *Volpone* and edited a new performing score for the Jerome Kern musical *Oh, Boy!* Day has served as music director for productions at City Lit and across the Chicago area. His new reconstruction of Chopin's last mazurka is published by Hal Leonard's Schirmer Performance Editions series, and he has given presentations on the piece at the Eastman School of Music, the Oberlin Conservatory of Music, Northwestern University, Lawrence University, Wesleyan University, and the University of Oklahoma. Day is the resident director for the Savoyaires, a Chicago-area Gilbert & Sullivan company that produced his original one-act *Six Characters in Search of Gilbert & Sullivan* and where he played the patter baritone lead in all fourteen G&S operettas. He has also been seen in such roles as Scrooge in *A Christmas Carol*, Sir Harcourt Courtly in *London Assurance*, Charlie Baker in *The Foreigner*, and Terry in *Casa Valentina*. Day has written extensively for publications by Northwestern University, where he was lead publications editor in the Office of Global Marketing and Communications.

ALSO FROM THE MENTORIS PROJECT

America's Forgotten Founding Father
A Novel Based on the Life of Filippo Mazzei
by Rosanne Welch, PhD

A. P. Giannini—Il Banchiere di Tutti
di Francesca Valente

A. P. Giannini—The People's Banker
by Francesca Valente

The Architect Who Changed Our World
A Novel Based on the Life of Andrea Palladio
by Pamela Winfrey

At Last
A Novel Based on the Life of Harry Warren
by Stacia Raymond

A Boxing Trainer's Journey
A Novel Based on the Life of Angelo Dundee
by Jonathan Brown

Breaking Barriers
A Novel Based on the Life of Laura Bassi
by Jule Selbo

Building Heaven's Ceiling
A Novel Based on the Life of Filippo Brunelleschi
by Joe Cline

Building Wealth
From Shoeshine Boy to Real Estate Magnate
by Robert Barbera

Building Wealth 101
How to Make Your Money Work for You
by Robert Barbera

Character is What Counts
A Novel Based on the Life of Vince Lombardi
by Jonathan Brown

Christopher Columbus: His Life and Discoveries
by Mario Di Giovanni

Dark Labyrinth
A Novel Based on the Life of Galileo Galilei
by Peter David Myers

Defying Danger
A Novel Based on the Life of Father Matteo Ricci
by Nicole Gregory

Desert Missionary
A Novel Based on the Life of Father Eusebio Kino
by Nicole Gregory

The Divine Proportions of Luca Pacioli
A Novel Based on the Life of Luca Pacioli
by W.A.W. Parker

The Dream of Life
A Novel Based on the Life of Federico Fellini
by Kate Fuglei

Dreams of Discovery
A Novel Based on the Life of the Explorer John Cabot
by Jule Selbo

The Embrace of Hope
A Novel Based on the Life of Frank Capra
by Kate Fuglei

The Faithful
A Novel Based on the Life of Giuseppe Verdi
by Collin Mitchell

Fermi's Gifts
A Novel Based on the Life of Enrico Fermi
by Kate Fuglei

The Pirate Prince of Genoa
A Novel Based on the Life of Admiral Andrea Doria
by Maurizio Marmorstein

Relentless Visionary: Alessandro Volta
by Michael Berick

Retire and Refire
Simple Financial Strategies to Navigate Your Best Years with Ease
by Robert Barbera

Ride Into the Sun
A Novel Based on the Life of Scipio Africanus
by Patric Verrone

Rita Levi-Montalcini
Pioneer & Ambassador of Science
by Francesca Valente

Saving the Republic
A Novel Based on the Life of Marcus Cicero
by Eric D. Martin

The Seven Senses of Italy
by Nicole Gregory